BOOK ONE OF T...

FATE'S
HAND

by
MELISSA MACFIE

Kelly Anne,
Enjoy the book!
— Melissa Macfie

Can't Put It Down Books
An Imprint of
Open Door Publications

Fate's Hand
Book One of The Celtic Prophecy
Copyright 2015 by Melissa Macfie

ISBN: 978-0-9972024-0-3
Printed in the United States of America

This is a work of fiction. Names, characters, places and incidents are either a product of the author's imagination or are used fictitiously. Any resemblance to actual events, or persons or locales, living or dead, is purely coincidental.

Published by
Can't Put It Down Books
An imprint of
Open Door Publications
2113 Stackhouse Dr.
Yardley, PA 19067

Cover Design by Genevieve Lavo Cosdon, lavodesign.com

This book is dedicated to my parents, Thomas and Nancy Hughes, who taught me that the only limits there are in this world are the ones you give yourself.

*When a thing is first conceived all things are possible;
but only when a choice is made, does fate take a hand.*

TABLE OF CONTENTS

PROLOGUE

The Oracle, the most revered and feared of the Vates, cocked her head, her milky white eye rounding on the dying man. She dropped to a predatory crouch, the ragged shawl resettling around her shoulders like ruffled feathers, its ends trailing on the ground, soaking up the spreading blood. She patted his hand, giving the man some solace, helping him to die, when she had set him on this path. Unaware that her succor flowed from a poisoned teat, the deluded bastard scrambled to get closer to her, but his arms and legs found no purchase on the ground slick with his blood.

Cormac MacBrehon's stomach heaved, but he turned away too late, glimpsing her poking at the exposed intestines, leaning closer, hooked nose almost touching—

"What the fuck is taking so long?"

Momentarily relieved that his morbid trance was broken, he glanced aside and read the impatience etched in the clenched fists and the cords that stuck out from the acolyte's scrawny neck. Relief soured into rage. "Death, then rigor mortis." He had to fight back an urge to snap the boy's spine at his blank, puzzled countenance still after eighty years of lessons. "In time," he instructed, more for himself than his student. "Several more hours, a' least, because th' weather is unseasonably warm."

"Fuck patience." The novice rounded on him to stand just inches away from his face, "Master, we've waited long enough. The time to strike is now. The prophecies have decreed it."

"Insolent bastard," thought Cormac. If only he were free to act. "Hmm and how d'ye propose we dae tha'? We doonae ken whaur ta begin."

"And you want to let this, this..." sweeping his hand in the direction of the old woman, "this thing dictate..."

Fury spilling over, adrenaline pumping, he seized his student's neck; it would be easy to snap the fragile bones under his fingers. Pressure in just the right spot and...lift...blood pooling in the boy's face...such a lovely shade of purple. He relished the dawning submission in the boy's eyes and smiled, his temper leveling. So unsuspecting, so naïve the young are; part of their nature, to have this illusion of invulnerability that blinds them to danger. "Hold yer tongue, laddie. And for all 'tis holy, keep yer voice doon."

The boy scrabbled at the ground trying to find a toehold, anything that would keep his weight on the ground as he clawed at the imprisoning hand.

Cormac squeezed again to educate; the student does not instruct the teacher.

Audible gasping gave way to breathless grunts, and the fumbling fingers lost their urgency. Hands flailed, but the fingers caressed, and once he saw respect reflected in the dying eyes, he released his grip. The boy stumbled away choking, gasping for breath. He stood over him, "Or I might volunteer ye ta be th' next ta receive her attentions."

The acolyte cringed, crawling away but keeping his teacher and the Oracle in sight.

"No' so daft then. Perhaps ye'r learning after all these years." He walked away, turning his back on the boy.

As Master Bard, Cormac's duties were to serve as a living anthology for the Order, but his skill set lay particularly with extracting secrets. Mandated to pass along the office to his descendants, his secret, the most prized of all, was that it was all for naught; he had no intention of leaving—ever.

The bard looked at the Oracle still squatting by the body, dipping her fingers in entrails, using the blood as ink to scribe Ogham symbols at equidistant points around the sacrifice. He needed her for now. Her methods were unpleasant, but he would bring people in droves—lambs to the slaughter, willing or no. He would even participate in the eviscerations if it would help clear the murky visions. Frustration bubbled up from his impotence to bring matters to a close. Bound by dictates created by the elders, it was not his jurisdiction yet, for that he had to rely on this brazen pup.

"If ye are no' pleased wi' th' progress," eyeing the acolyte still crumpled on the ground, "then I suggest ye lift th' strictures put on her. Interpreting signs would be verra much easier with a group as opposed ta only one. Thaur is no' much she can glean from one."

The boy sat up and coughed to clear his throat, but his voice was strained still, "It is my appointed task...hu humph...to ascertain...uh, the threat from the authorities

3

before we're set to move. Humph. I have done that...done that for centuries, uh hmphm."

"Aye, but by yer own assessment, we are no closer ta finding th' priestess. Perhaps 'tis not th' fault o' th' Vate's, but yer own."

Clearing his throat, he spit, "Do you not remember England? The barn? Careful plans were laid; a false history was planted for the Wickerman's volunteers. Chalk it all up to zealotry, but it all went to shit—turned into a fucking charnel house!" The boy paced away and then turned. "Do you know or care how difficult it was for me to cover up the remnants of the ritual? The fire did not burn hot enough to turn all evidence to ash, the remains of thirty-three people, contorted in the last throes of death."

Cormac crossed his arms and leaned against the portico's upright post. "Ye concocted th' plan and built th' Wickerman inside tha' abandoned barn. Did ye no' think th' barn would be engulfed?"

"Do I look stupid? Don't answer that. You know that I planned for that, but she refused to allow the use of the accelerant."

"And ye verra well ken why. Gasoline raises th' temperature o' th' flame, incinerating th' delicacy o' th' sacrifice. She takes in everythin', th' time it takes for th' sacrifice ta be overcome, th' height and temperature o' th' flames, th' length o' th' burn, th' weather conditions, th' behavior o' th' surrounding fauna; and all this afore readin' th' final omen," he pointed to the body, "th' results such as those yonder."

"We cannot continue in this fashion for the likes of a

4

seer, no matter her power in divination."

"T'was through her divination we narrowed th' search. Afore th' Wickerman incident we would ha' been better served looking for th' proverbial needle in a haystack. We noo ha' a time and a location.

"Granted, but we are fighting two battles. The more sensational the rituals are, the more likely it is that they will garner public attention. The priestess needs to be found quietly. If the entire Order is made aware of her existence in this time we won't be able to get our hands on her. She'll be heavily guarded with sycophants who have elevated her position to that of messiah. She is a mere woman."

Cormac nodded. It was true, she was just a woman, but her potential was legendary, thanks to prophecy and augury, a vulnerable woman with the power to topple a god.

"In our efforts to find her quickly and quietly, technology—forensic science—has advanced even though your thinking hasn't. All it would take would be one fingerprint, one piece of DNA thoughtlessly left behind to give the authorities a lead they have been champing for to send them directly to us. Wanton actions such as these have dire consequences now."

"T'was easy for ye, if I remember correctly, ta pass off th' charnel house as religious zealotry. A group who in yer words, though I doonae understand th' reference, 'Drank their own brand o' Kool-Aid,' I ken it was. Aye?"

"Do your own damned research. In fact, why don't you adapt like the rest of us? Live in the times, perhaps?"

Eyebrow raised, Cormac scoffed, and advanced on his

apprentice, who sat back on the retaining wall. The boy tried to cringe back but the bard grabbed his sweatshirt and hoisted him up, "Like ye, I suppose. Go ta university; get an education and a measly job, doin' wha'? Hm? Ye say ye work in guise only, but yer nothin' more than cattle. Settle down, get a wife, impregnate her? Th' only minutely appealing thing 'tis th' ever so brief relief I'd find between some cow's legs. Thaur'll be tha' in abundance soon. Whate'er I want, I'll take.

"As for diverting th' attentions o' th' authorities, tha' falls to ye, too. And believe me when I tell ye, if necessary, ye will take th' fall for this. Let yerself be captured, imprisoned, and put ta death if necessary, all ta ensure th' fruition o' our plans."

Scuffling attracted their attention in time to see the Oracle scuttle to the head of her victim as he burbled the last of his breath, mouth thick with blood. Satisfied, she sat back on her haunches and sniffed the air. Her head turned and the milky eye pierced them, growing wide as if she had just realized they were in attendance.

The creaking of joints echoed in the portico as the Oracle ambled barefoot through the pool of blood unheeding, leaving the corpse unattended. Cormac grabbed the acolyte and held fast as she approached, with arms locked outstretched, shackling his offering, a human shield. Take him. Take him.

The woman was of small stature, a homunculus, made even smaller by the hump on her back. She jabbed the arrogant boy in the belly, hard enough to make him bend in reflex, then she grabbed his chin and pulled his face close to hers. Fingertips dug in, leaving bloody smears on his jaw.

"Impatient, are ye? I ha' a mind ta take yer instructor's advice." She clawed at the sweatshirt, pushing it up so his rib cage was exposed. The knife appeared out of the voluminous folds of her cloak, still bloody, and pressed into his flesh. Visibly excited by the welling of blood, she angled the knife and sliced ever so lightly along the rib cage. A thin line of blood followed the blade, and the boy hissed through his teeth. "Ye bleed well."

The bard offered, "If t'would help, take him. I ha' other apprentices." He knew full well that she wouldn't, a slave to prophecy herself, but the just the idea of silencing the arrogance once and for all gave him some release.

"Ye ken better than I tha' I cannae. It has been deemed tha' whaur wha' will, must be. We are no' ta question." Motioning to Cormac, "However, the lad requires a lesson. Bring him."

Careful to avoid her bloody footprints, they reached the side of the body. She was the Oracle, but had the vanity of a woman nonetheless. What did one say for this? Cormac settled, "Nicely done," as he swiftly kicked the back of his novice's knee, forcing the boy down closer to the body. Keeping a heavy hand on each shoulder, "Teach him wha' ye will."

Instead of directing his gaze to the corpse in front of him as Cormac expected her to do, she sat next to the acolyte and shooed his hands off the boy's shoulders, dismissing him like a schoolboy. He had no choice but to step back and just observe, fuming at her impudence. She was the angel of mercy to the initiates who all but clamored

7

to sacrifice themselves at her hands. She was doting and patient, allowing the acolyte to absorb the information at his own pace. To Cormac, though, she was someone to be feared; the eye, the dead eye, followed him, looking into his soul to extract his secrets.

She patted the boy's hand, "Leuk around ye, laddie. Tell me wha' ye see."

"What? Um...I don't know. Wall of the house there, roof of the carport overhead..."

"Leuk deeper," she interrupted.

"Some household supplies there by the wall, old paint cans, a dented and rusted garbage can, empty, an upturned gasoline canister for a lawnmower which is just beyond in the high grass, a broken window there, yellow paint peeling off the wooden ledge."

"Aye. Tell me more."

"Unpruned trees are overhanging the gravel driveway almost indistinct amongst the infiltrating weeds. No sound of traffic, children, or car doors closing, just the chatter of birds in the trees."

"Wha' does this tell ye?"

"Um... no one cares for the property?" He looked at her expectantly.

"True, but if ye were payin' attention, when the initiate was first cut he made enough noise ta scatter those birds. But they didna fly. They remained thaur, hopping from branch to branch searching out food or minding their eggs, unconcerned about th' skelloch haur. Can ye learn anything from tha'?"

Looking up at the tree, behind at his teacher, and then

back to the woman, "I don't know."

"Well, 'tis only one o' th' signs, th' first o' many. We are in th' right land ta search for her. If they flew, of course, depending on th' length of their flight, it would mean tha' we are searching in th' wrong place, time, or even both. But they stayed. Th' birds' behavior is not th' only factor for this determination, though. Leuk at th' body o' th' initiate."

"Ugh." The skin was peeled back from sternum to groin revealing the peritoneum, which was cut delicately down the center exposing the bulging intestines, which showed no outward sign of breach.

"Wha' can ye tell me about this?"

"Ugh, the human body reeks."

She laughed. "Och, aye. A natural smell." Sniffing close to him, "Much like body odor is a sign o' life, this is a sign o' decay. It happens quickly. But this is no' th' answer I want. Leuk closer. Dae ye have th' basic knowledge o' human anatomy?"

"A little." Pointing, "Large intestine, small intestine."

"Tis sufficient. Give me observations."

He shied away, turning his body as if deciding to deny the corpse's existence, and closed his eyes, but he did as she asked, holding out an arm, vaguely gesticulating to observations obviously scarred in his memory. "Um, the large intestine is kinda bunched up there towards the top, while that length of small intestine is out of its cavity and draped a bit on the ground next to him."

The Vate gripped his outstretched hand and forced it into the pile of innards. He violently resisted. Cormac moved to intervene, but she motioned him to stay where he was. "Tis more than thirty feet o' intestine in th' human body and once th' sac tha' holds th' intestines is pierced, it usually spills out, but haur, it didna, despite th' initiate's writhing on th' ground. Only this small section," holding it up reverently, "escaped its bonds."

"What does that mean?"

Cormac could hear the strain in his voice, and for a brief moment he felt for the kid. He didn't know, if situations were reversed, if he'd be able to keep his stomach down. Better the acolyte than him. Killing was easy, he relished the power he felt, more each time, but this just seemed a sacrilege, even though it was warranted. Killing slowly; there was only one person he'd love to have the opportunity to see writhe, beg for mercy, of which he'd receive none.

"Th' birds' behavior taken inta account with this sign, we are close. She will no' be difficult ta track doon noo."

The novice looked back at the body, perplexed, "How did you come to that conclusion?"

"The intestines ha' stayed inside, indicating tha' we are in th' right geographic location. Mind ye, just taking this inta account, it means we are in th' same general vicinity. According ta distance measures, it could still mean tha' we are off by several hundred miles yet. But take inta account tha' nay other living things, including th' birds, were bothered by th' disturbance haur, indicates further tha' we are verra close ta our conquest." She felt the limbs of the body. "Good. Th' stiffening has begun." She got to her feet using his shoulder. "Come."

He stood and followed to stand several feet away; his teacher approached to stand at his side.

"Stay haur and observe."

The woman pivoted away and circled the body, chanting low. Cormac couldn't hear her, and if he read his novice's face accurately, neither could he. It was intentional on the part of the Oracle. It was the end of her revelations into augury.

She circled the body, trailing over the painted Ogham symbols, and after the second revolution each symbol glowed with white incandescence when she passed. With the completion of her second turn the drying blood that had spilled from the initiate's body glowed, and with the speed of one much younger, the Vate swooped in to take the head between her hands and breathe in the expulsion of trapped air that escaped from the dead man's unmoving mouth. With that last expulsion of gas the body convulsed and grew rigid, heels planted into the ground, back bowed so the head came to rest at a sharp upward angle. She raised her head, eyes glowing with fire, "I ha' found th' high priestess."

CHAPTER 1

Brenawyn McAllister swallowed the bile forcing its way up as she passed the 97th mile marker on the New Jersey turnpike. She slowed to let a tractor-trailer block her view of the mangled guardrail, but nothing stopped the surfacing images of the Jeep, a grotesquely twisted, blackened husk once representing a life. Liam's.

A slave to the demands of routine, her eyes were riveted to the rearview mirror's reflection before the truck had cleared it. This was the last time she would pass here, and she needed to see one last time. The tattered tails of a faded yellow ribbon tied to the rusted metal, a ribbon that she had tied there, snapped taut in the wind as the truck passed, a beacon screaming "traitor."

It was three fucking years ago.

It was yesterday.

To learn about the accident through empty platitudes, and later through the report that mocked her in its factual clarity, it gave her no release, no closure.

Breathe.

Her nightmares were enough. Living here, passing here every day, was too much to bear. She had to get out or die alone.

Brenawyn watched the sunset from the George

Washington Bridge, the beginning of twenty-nine-mile bumper-to-bumper traffic with no surcease. By the time she crawled over the Connecticut border she itched for a moment's reprieve from her torture device to stretch her stiff back and cramped legs. The Challenger, with manual transmission, was one of her few splurges, but the pleasure of driving it was lost in the hours spent crawling along I-95.

The mile and half mile marker signs for the Darian rest stop taunted her. She could see it in the distance, its Golden Arches lit, as if from an ocean away. An hour later, she finally pulled into the only available spot in the parking lot. The vibrations of shifting gears woke Spencer and he jumped up and danced around the front seat. Brenawyn could barely hook the leash onto his collar.

"Hold still, dog. Oww! Stop stepping on me. Ouch! Remind me to get your nails trimmed."

Spencer licked her face and whined. "All right, I know. Five hours is a long time to be stuck in the car. I know. I have been stuck in here too. I couldn't help it, though." Throwing a glance back at the congested highway, "People who can't drive should stay home."

Yanked by her dog the second the car door opened, she swore that she'd leash train him yet, no matter how long it took. Tongue lolling out the side of his mouth, he pranced in circles around her, bumping her legs and stepping on her toes. Adjusting her hold on his lead, Brenawyn led him to the scalped grass.

Here, she let out the retractable leash enough to allow him to sniff everything within a five-foot range. She glanced around, her father's voice in her head—*always be aware of your surroundings, Bren*—and saw the odd shadows the cars cast in the poorly lit lot. Faceless silhouettes moved on missions to and from the building. Music thumped from an open car somewhere nearby; she could feel the bass in the soles of her feet. No one looked threatening. No one looked friendly, either.

"Okay, time to go, Spence." Turning around, she dragged the dog back to the car, opened the door, and struggled to get him in as he whined. "Just hush. I'll be right back."

She opened the restroom door and, a fetid odor hit her. Lazy gnats buzzed low over the stagnant water pooled beneath the sinks and around the toilets. She hesitated for a moment, considering her less than adequate foot attire. Why had she drunk the whole extra-large coffee in the car? It left her no choice but to brave the bathroom. "God, I hope that's water," she prayed as she navigated around the larger pools. She inspected the stalls—no paper, no paper, not flushed, no paper, God knows what on the seat, and no paper. Rooting around in her purse, Brenawyn excavated the last two tissues from their plastic sleeve. If only she had replaced them with a new pack before she left, though two were better than nothing. Choosing the first stall with no paper, Brenawyn closed herself within the small space.

The adjacent stall's hinges squeaked as she turned to flush the toilet with her foot. Hands braced on either side for balance, Brenawyn glimpsed an arthritic hand reaching under the stall wall. "I'm sorry, there is no extra paper in here. I had to use a tissue myself." But there was no other response than the hand withdrawing.

Brenawyn jumped and dropped her purse when a screech bellowed out from the adjacent stall. She knocked on the stall wall, concerned, but as she bent to retrieve her fallen bag, the gnarled hand darted under the wall again to clamp onto her ankle. Heart pounding, she pivoted and wrenched herself loose from the bony claw's vise-like grip.

The shrieking continued and the claw found her again. Shit, this was just the sort of thing her father had warned her about. She pulled the handle. The door didn't budge. Panicked, she yanked on it. Nothing. *The latch. Undo the latch first.* Brenawyn stomped on the wrist, feeling a wet pop reverberate through the sole of her shoe.

She flung the door open and dashed out. *I fall, I'm dead.* Her flip flops slipped and squeaked across the floor; she lost one along the way. She left it. She crashed into the door and pitched herself into the arms of an unsuspecting man walking into the shared restroom vestibule. "Are ye hurt, lass?"

Dazed, Brenawyn clutched the wall of muscle, finding brief comfort, and she looked up into bright blue eyes, but she had to get away. "Sorry. Don't go in there."

The safety of the car beckoned in the distance; Spencer was barking and clawing at the window. She threw her bag on the hood and frantically searched through it, dumping half its contents before she found her keys. She fumbled, her fingers stiff and awkward, before finally grabbing the keyless remote. Pressing both the unlock and panic buttons, she scooped up her purse, whisked the wallet, passport, and other junk strewn across the hood into the bag, and threw herself into the car, jabbing the buttons over and over again long after the first contact locked the doors. Spencer stood over her lap, hunched low, growling out the window.

The panic alarm screamed. No one in the packed lot paid attention. Finally finding the right button, she disengaged the alarm before she jammed the key into the ignition, started the car, and revved the engine. Wrestling the dog to the passenger seat, she didn't see the woman approach. Her head whipped to attention, eyes locked with the old hag as the car rocked from the impact of the woman's fists on the hood of the car.

"Shit." Brenawyn threw the gearshift in reverse without looking and careened out of the parking space, the smell of burnt rubber filling her nose. Spencer rushed into the backseat and growled at the woman.

Brenawyn craned her neck to get another look, but the woman was gone. A car horn blared and she slammed on her brakes seconds before plowing into the hag. She ripped through the gears as she threw the car into first. Twisting her neck to judge the distance, "What the fuck is going on?" Three hundred or more feet between the car and the parking space—no one could move that fast.

The old woman stood in the middle of the bypass road, cradling her arm, ignoring horns and screeching brakes. She raised her arms, the left wrist hanging at an impossible angle. Eyes glowing with red incandescence met Brenawyn's stare.

"Oh, hell no!" She popped the clutch and whipped the wheel to swerve around the woman.

A line of cars waiting for their chance to sit in traffic materialized beyond the building, but Brenawyn leaned on the horn and took the shoulder. Gravel hit the undercarriage like machine gun fire as she flew past the stopped cars at breakneck speed.

~ ~ ~

The car roared to life as she approached, and she could see by the quick punctuated movements of Cormac's shadowed figure that he was angry. She slid onto the passenger seat as quick as her joints would allow and was greeted by tension rolling off of the impertinent Bard. He stared ahead, slamming his hands against the steering wheel three times before throwing the gearshift in reverse.

She put her hand on his arm. "Och, let her go," she asserted.

He pivoted in his seat to face her, shaking his head, "Wha'?"

"We need ta think and organize in light o' this new development. Go ta th' hotel. I need ta consult th' prophecies."

"But—"

She interrupted, "Ye will respect me, child. Doonae think I forgot tha' ye were willing ta give up yer apprentice so easily." She scrutinized him sitting there, knowing he needed to be reminded of his place. "I wonder wha' kind o' picture ye would paint for me with yer own blud."

He lowered his eyes, shrinking away from her in the confines of the car. She leaned toward him and whispered, "Thaur is nay prophecy concerning ye, and if 'tis required of him ta be th' scapegoat, perhaps it falls ta ye ta become my *next* volunteer."

He drew back further, disjointedly, until his head made

17

a satisfying clunk against the closed window. It took a moment longer, too long for her tastes, for the fight to go out of his frame. Perhaps the time was coming to show him his place.

"Call in th' Shaman," she demanded.

"I doonae like him."

"Yer opinion wasna asked. Call him."

"He's irrevocably set in his ways."

"Yes, and we will use tha'. Th' priestess needs ta be found and we ken who she is." She looked out at the parking lot, contemplating her next words before continuing. "We are no' th' only ones looking for her."

"Aye, but if he learns o' our plans?"

"How much ye disclose is yer decision. Ye seem no' ta trust him, but yer reasoning holds verra little interest ta me. Tell him enough ta find who is responsible for dropping th' veil."

"We doonae need Sinclair."

She disregarded his obstinacy. "He'll be compelled ta take up th' mantle and destroy whoe'er stands in th' way. Once she is found, Cernunnos will call th' Shaman back ta th' Stalking Grounds, making him impotent ta interfere with our plans."

"Thaur is no way for him ta escape once thaur?"

The Oracle sighed. "Even if thaur was, he has nay soul, thanks ta yer acolyte's hoor. She made sure ta destroy his reliquary. He only exists through his connection ta th' Wild Hunt, but he is th' Shaman. He will be released on th' four days o' adoration when his participation is required, but then will be at th' mercy of th' Wild Hunt for rest o' th' wheel o' time."

"Those four days are enough ta disrupt my—our—designs." Cormac protested.

"Patience, my child. Only 'til Saimhain will we be vulnerable."

CHAPTER 2

The shoulder opened a bit when the acceleration lanes gave way to the highway. Bypassing agitated drivers, a few cars followed Brenawyn's lead on the shoulder, and twenty minutes later, she passed the last of highway construction. Roaring past, ignoring workers as they yelled and waved at the cavalcade of cars, she shifted into fifth gear. The more distance between herself and the old woman, the more the knot eased in her chest.

Spencer turned from the back window and shook himself, lather flying. He didn't sit, but poked his upper body between the seats to perch partially on the console, standing watch, his jowl stuck on an exposed canine.

Brenawyn now noticed the dashboard plastic peeled away like paper straw wrappers, and the frothy saliva drying on the windshield. Claw marks punctuated by—she looked down at the dog's paws—dry blood.

The car ate up the highway, and by the time the Salem welcome sign appeared on the horizon, Brenawyn had trouble discerning the truth from figments of her tired imagination. Thrown off by the state of the unkempt bathroom, the woman probably just wanted toilet paper. Perhaps she couldn't hear, or spoke another language? The woman's red eyes were definitely her wild imagination's doing, and the distance from the parking spot to the bypass road a perception issue. But the dog's response?

As if hearing it would make it be so, she said, "Yep, that's it, I'm just tired." Catching sight of Spencer's reflection in the rearview mirror, "Don't look at me like that. It was just my imagination and that's that!"

Brenawyn turned the corner, and the car's headlights did nothing to illuminate the long shadows on her grandmother's familiar street. She slid into a parking spot in front of The Rising Moon, the establishment her grandmother owned. The store's windows were dark, as were those of the residence above. It was too early to announce her arrival, but lights shone from the bakery across the street, as if calling all ships home. *Not too early for fresh croissants.*

As the car door swung wide, the offending lone flip flop slapped the pavement, reminding her to retrieve her antibacterial wipes from the glove compartment. She rubbed several pads on her feet and donned another pair of dollar store sandals that she grabbed from the backseat. "Kills ninety-nine percent of bacteria—it will have to do until I can scrub my skin off."

She shuddered as she bent to grab the discarded flip flop, holding it at arm's length between two fingertips while trying to handle the dog that bolted out of the car like a rushing tidal wave. He crashed into the door, making it strain against its hinges, and she lurched as the dog tripped her, fumbling the shoe.

"God damn it, dog," rubbing her stubbed toe. "It's combat boots for me from now on." Retrieving it again and hobbling on her injured foot, she tossed it into the nearest trashcan on the curb.

Spencer took two steps and sniffed the air. His hackles rose and he moved in front of Brenawyn, herding her with his bottom in the direction of the car. Brenawyn looked into the deep shadows afforded by the broken streetlamp halfway down the block. "Jesus." She stepped around him and yanked on his lead. He fought, his nails scrabbling on the asphalt, choking on the strained collar, but she won and hurried across the street to the safety of the lighted, public bakery.

~ ~ ~

Alexander Sinclair was among the few midnight denizens who stalked the bakery for freshly baked bread. He had to remember to eat. Tonight, following a lead, he had slogged through miles of construction traffic tailing the mark, only to be led to a rest stop, where it appeared for an instant that his search would finally bear fruit, but he was too damned eager.

The Oracle was there again, as she always was: the shadow, the tool of his nemesis. What her name was, where she came from, it didn't matter. She was *The Oracle*. The enemy was getting bolder, using her for other than interpreting omens—he was desperate. Time was running out. Never before had she made direct contact. Alexander wouldn't have believed it had he not seen her slam her fists on the hood of that car, nor sift time to appear again, an obstacle barring the escape route. From his perch, he had done what he could for the fleeing woman, casting a spell, bringing down the veil between worlds for a fraction of a second, enough to set the dog off in warning.

This time, it had been enough.

He couldn't be seen taking action in direct opposition to the Order. Theirs—his—was a holy mission, to hold the balance until the Priestess was revealed. But he knew after centuries even the most devout could be tempted. Convincing the elders of this, most of whom turned a blind eye to the corruption that fractured the group, was an insurmountable feat. They refused to believe that one could be turned by avarice.

Brought out of his ruminations by the appearance of headlights turning the corner, his instincts screamed until he activated his runes and stepped back into enhanced shadows. The car door opened. What were the odds that the very woman he had saved tonight was coming here, less than a block from where he lived?

Alex started at the dog's growl—interesting that the dog was so attuned to magic. He took a few steps to the curb, unwilling to leave cover completely lest his concealment be discovered. He squatted, touched the asphalt with his fingertips and waited for his spell to move through the man-made material to reach the dog across the street. The dog quieted within seconds.

He watched the woman cross to the bakery, choose a table near the entrance, and tie the unruly dog's leash to the bars of the wrought iron fence. He waited until she went in and then sprinted across the street. The two dents on the hood confirmed what he already knew to be true.

He had to meet her, talk with her, learn if she was a likely candidate; but it would be counterproductive if he scared her. He knew what she'd see—a large, hulking man. So when the woman emerged with a Styrofoam cup and a brown paper bag, it was to find Alex petting her dog. Animals had a way of disarming people. He could see she was surprised to find him there. She hesitated a moment, scanned the area, and then approached, depositing the cup and bag on the table.

Alexander focused on the dog, speaking Gaelic nonsense to it before looking up and taking in a lovely view of her toned calves. The sight ended slightly above her knees where the lace trim of her shift—her dress—started. She was tall for a woman, with a figure that made a man's hands ache to hold.

"Good morning."

Alex flashed a smile and stood, despite the dog's protests at the sudden neglect. She had a mass of dark hair tied into a floppy knot on top of her head, with wisps falling around her shoulders. "Oh, haló. Nice animal ye ha'. Well-built and friendly." He patted the dog one last time. "I am Alexander Sinclair." Taking a step toward her, he held out his hand.

Wide eyes, as green as new grass before a storm, met his gaze. The woman's stance changed, posture straight, feet spread slightly apart, and her eyes darted to the open gate, aware of the change in the environment his presence made, but she took the hand that he offered, "Brenawyn McAllister, nice to meet you."

Modern woman, indeed, but at least she was aware of potential danger, even if she wasn't conscious of that fact. She felt his power, even if she'd likely define it as the ability to command a room; Alex had his work cut out for him. "I'll leave ye to yer breakfast," and entered the bakery. When he emerged, she was still there, half concealed by the trellised vines, hair down now, spilling in glossy thickness over her shoulder as she bent to scratch behind the dog's ear.

He stopped with his back toward her and took a careful sip of the coffee, savoring its richness, then took a bigger swig. She cleared her throat, and he looked in her direction as she brought her cup halfway to her lips, "It's good here. You should try the croissants too."

He held up the bag.

She took a fortifying sip of her coffee, "Um…if you're not in a hurry, would you like to share the table?"

He looked around the courtyard at the six other empty tables. "Certainly," he pulled out the chair opposite her. The dog cried to get closer to him. Alex asked, "So wha' kind o' dog is he?"

Brenawyn looked down, and leaned over to untangle the leash from the table legs, giving him an unobstructed view of her ample cleavage. "Oh, Spencer's a pit bull mix that I rescued from a shelter two years ago. I walked in and he jumped in my arms from a desk in the middle of the room. The clerk had been trying to put him in a cage when I walked in. I fell in love instantly. I didn't listen to the man try to talk me out of adopting him even while I was signing the papers." Rubbing Spencer's head, "The best dog I have ever had. Looks ferocious, but he's all mush. Aren't you boy?"

Alexander took another sip of his coffee, "Seems

friendly. Ye made a good choice. Are ye haur on vacation or just passing through?"

"Neither. I'm relocating here. I'm going to stay with family until I can find a suitable place to live, but I'm in no rush." Brenawyn answered. "It is a little too early to announce my arrival, but then I remembered this place. It's much better than any franchised coffee shop."

"And definitely better than any rest stop."

At the mention of rest stops, Brenawyn straightened a fraction. Fear, anxiety, and curiosity flashed in turn on her face and she shook her head.

Eyebrows raised, Alex asked, "Wha's th' trouble, lass?"

"Oh, noth…" She stopped and cocked her head to the side, considering him with slightly squinted eyes. "It's nothing...just, that's the second time tonight that I've been called lass."

Alex sat, schooling his face to show no emotion, no reaction to what she said.

"Huh," shaking her head, "The imagination is working overtime. Nothing a good night's sleep won't cure."

Noting the time it took for her features to change from wary to relaxed, he assessed her to be a product of contemporary society, where everything has a logical explanation. She was confident, not one to over-deliberate on issues, albeit drawing the wrong conclusions, making his task all the more complicated. Her naiveté would make her an easy target, and quite possibly by the time she was convinced that not everything neatly conformed to her expectation of logic, it might be too late for intervention.

He drank the last of his coffee and stood up, leaving the bag untouched. "It was nice talking with ye, and welcome ta th' neighborhood."

Brenawyn stood up and held her hand out. Alexander took it and curled her fingers around his own, brought it to his lips. "My friends call me Alex. I hope I can count ye among them."

Brenawyn nodded as he walked away. Alex could feel her eyes upon him. He never had difficulty attracting women. It seemed a bit hollow to use his appeal to lead her on, but time was against him. Looking back over his shoulder, he gave her his sexiest smile, "I will see you again, *a chuisle.*[1]"

~~~

Alex trudged up the stairs, entered his second floor apartment, and slammed the door closed. Something was wrong. The wards protecting his place were shattered and the defensive spells nullified.

"Ye ken, someone could slip a knife between yer ribs or slit yer throat while ye try ta piece togeth'r facts. No' me, of course, but someone."

Alex sprang to face the intruder, knowing the safety of his home was compromised. The man sat reclining in a cushioned chair with feet up, crossed at the ankle on the coffee table. Cormac was several inches shorter than Alex. While lithe and fairly capable of handling himself in a fight, he could never take Alex. He wore his shoulder length blonde hair clubbed at the nape, as usual. There was that

---

[1] My heart

usual smug look set into his wide brow and jaw that Alex thought a good beating would wipe away.

"Cormac." Alex relaxed slightly and turned his back, reaching for the kitchen towel on the counter to wipe his face. "To wha' dae I owe th' pleasure o' yer company?" He leaned back against the counter that separated the kitchen from the living space and tossed the towel into the sink.

"Th' Oracle needs ye ta deal with certain…difficulties, as we try ta obtain th' target."

"Obtain th' target? Hm. I doona care for yer word choice, Cormac. Get oot o' my house."

Cormac stood, dusting off his trousers, "Doonae ye want ta ken th' particulars?"

Instinct told Alex to throw him out, but reason stayed his hand. He had to know what they knew, what they suspected. "Aye. Wha' does she want me ta dae?"

"Closing in on th' target tonight, someone intervened on behalf o' th' woman, allowing her ta escape. Th' Oracle wants ye ta find th' source o' tha' interference and silence it."

"I'm no' a soldier ta be commanded, Cormac. I will leuk inta it, but as for intervening, I make th' decisions. Wha' form did this interference take?"

"Nothing overt. The veil dropped, for a moment. But it ha' th' finesse o' one of us."

"Ye think thaur's a traitor in our midst?"

Cormac crossed to the room and opened the unlatched door, "Tha' is yers ta figure out. I doona ha' ta tell ye how important it is."

"Still touched with impertinence I see. When this is

28

over, I'd love th' chance ta meet ye on th' Hunting Grounds ta teach ye proper respect."

Cormac chuckled, "Alas, my friend, tha' will ne'er be possible," as he closed the door behind him.

CHAPTER 3

By the time she had finished her cup of coffee, two lighted windows shone from the floors above the Rising Moon. She called, and by the time she had untied Spencer and walked across the street, her grandmother was waiting at the door.

"Pussy Cat, I'm so glad you're here. I've missed you."

"I've missed you too, Nana." The dog pranced around them, binding them together with his leash, "Spencer, stop! Be a good boy."

The dog knew the routine and lost interest the moment the leash was relinquished. He bounded into the foyer and up the stairs, clawing and whining at the upper door. "How was your ride? I guess you hit traffic. I was expecting you last night."

"The traffic was terrible, a never-ending crawl, thanks to construction all the way through New York and into Connecticut. I'm glad I won't be traveling that way again soon. What a nightmare!"

"Ugh, well at least it's over and you're here. Come in and get settled."

Brenawyn climbed the stairs after her grandmother, noting the brace on her right foot. "Nana, what happened?"

Stopping at the landing to open the door to let Spencer in, Leo looked down and held her foot out, "Oh, nothing really. The body is not what it used to be. I tripped over a box and landed wrong on my ankle. It will be better in a few days. I have a doctor's appointment later on today to get it checked out. Would you be able to drive me there?"

"Whatever you need."

Leoncha Callahan was a striking woman. Soft brown hair, which never saw the contents of a Clairol box, flowed over her shoulders. Bright blue eyes stared out of a face almost devoid of wrinkles. *God,* Brenawyn thought, *please let me have her genes.*

Her grandmother's age showed in subtle ways, though. Originally a tall woman, Leo's shoulders slumped, making the slight hump on her back more prominent. Her velour bed jacket and cotton nightgown hung on her. Had she lost more weight? Or was it just the perceived vulnerability of catching her in pajamas?

"Well, I know it's not what anyone has in mind for the first day of vacation, taking their aged grandmother to the doctor."

"Aged grandmother. Please stop. If that's where you need to go, I'll take you. Tripping over a box? Let me guess. Inventory?" Not needing confirmation, Brenawyn continued, "Why won't you let someone else do that for you? You could have ended up really hurting yourself."

Leo reached for and patted Brenawyn's hand, "Well now, dear, that's what I have you for, now. Don't I?" Leo let go and walked into her apartment, "I have homemade blueberry muffins for you if you're still hungry."

"Ooh yes, some dog, not mentioning any names, stole my croissant." The fuzzy culprit chose that moment to reenter the room and settle, after a few revolutions on the hearth rug.

"Certainly you're not referring to that cute and properly behaved boy who's resting so sweetly by the hearth?

"No, of course not. Not Spencer."

Brenawyn walked into the living room and placed her hand on the back of the pale pink floral couch and closed her eyes. She inhaled scents of lavender, sage, and something that was uniquely her grandmother. She was eight again, with corkscrew pig tails, clutching her teddy bear, the first time she ever was here. So many years ago and countless times since, she had stood in this very spot. The familiar smells were a comfort, and the occasional run-in with déjà vu always brought a smile to her lips. She never felt truly happy or completely safe unless she was in this exact spot. Looking around at her grandmother's collectibles, feeling a sense of wholeness, she knew she had made the right decision to come here for good.

"Come into the kitchen, when you're ready. Do you want butter on the muffin?"

"Plain would be fine."

"Are you sure? They are still warm from the oven."

"Ooh, on second thought, yes, butter would be great." She walked into the kitchen with the drink tray from the bakery. The white Battenberg lace placemats had been removed from the table and a muffin, cut in four equal pieces, each buttered, lay on a plate. Brenawyn picked up one of the pieces and took a bite. "Mm. Yummy," she said with her mouth full. "No one cooks like you, Nana."

"Thank you. I gave you the recipe years ago."

"True, but you put extra love in them."

"You're sweet." Putting her hand on Brenawyn's, "Dear, I'm so glad you're here, but are you sure you did the right thing, uprooting everything, job, house, friends, and everything in between?"

"Tell me, how does anyone know if they've done the right thing? Friends, my true friends, yes, I will miss them, but it's not as if I saw them on a regular basis anymore. Husbands, kids, jobs, responsibility...basically life, gets in the way. That goes for everyone. I'll still keep in contact with them with phone calls, email, birthday and holiday cards, and even the occasional vacation. Believe me, Maria will be here with her family before too long. Her kids are so big. Did I tell you she's pregnant again?"

"She is? How wonderful!"

Brenawyn nodded. "This move will be good for me. Getting away from Jersey, I feel like it's time to finally start over without constant reminders. Passing it every day on my way into work... how could anyone not remember? But I tried, you know I did. You helped me go through the house and his belongings, but there was still a sense of him; the chair that he would sit in after a long day and fall asleep, how he arranged his tools in the toolbox, and the hundreds of other things that all the rearranging of furniture wouldn't take away.

"I know what you mean. It's the reason I don't spend much time at the farmhouse."

"I'm sorry, Nana. Here I am going on as if I'm the only one who's ever lost a husband."

"That's all right, Pussy Cat."

"It's funny what sticks in your mind after someone dies: the name of the shade of lipstick that Mom wore, how Aunt Mary would roll down her knee-high stockings and bunch her pants about the knee when it was hot, or Liam's faded cut-off sweatpants, complete with a hole in the right leg."

Leo smiled slightly and looked out the window, "Memory is a strange thing," her mind clearly wrapped up in one of a thousand memories of her own.

CHAPTER 4

At 9:30, Leo retrieved the shop keys and headed to the connecting stairs beyond the kitchen. The front entrances to the store and the apartment above were separate, but the back stairs gave access to both spaces without having to go outside.

"Hold on, Nana. I'll come with you," Brenawyn called from the kitchen.

"Bah! Old age—can't do anything anymore! It's not necessary. I just have to go down to open the shop; Maggie will be coming shortly. She normally doesn't work until later on in the afternoon, but I asked her to come early today to mind the shop for me when we go to the doctor.

"But on second thought, come down. She'll see your car and won't stop pestering me with questions until she sees you."

Brenawyn came out of the kitchen, drying her hands on the back of her shorts, "Hold on, let me go first, these stairs are treacherous."

Leo knew where the concern came from, but it still rankled. How many years had she plowed down these stairs with no concern? Now, rickety stairs meant hazard to brittle bones. Brenawyn slowly descended the stairs, carefully attuned to Leo's steps, and they reached the bottom just as Maggie approached.

Brenawyn took the keys, and Leo could see through the full glass door that Maggie was bouncing on the balls of her feet in eager anticipation of being granted entrance. No sooner did Brenawyn get the keys out of the door than Maggie launched herself at her. "Oof"

"Ha, you're finally here. I never thought today would get here. This week dragged. How was your trip? Are you staying for the whole summer again? When can we hang out? Where is Spencer? Did you bring him? Of course you brought him. Where is he? There is a new flavor of iced cappuccino next door, we should get one later, then you can tell me everything that happened during the past year. Leave nothing out. Promise?"

Brenawyn hugged her back. "Whoa, easy, one question at a time." Holding the 19-year-old girl at arm's length, she shook her head and laughed. "You asked me so many questions that you lost me. It's good to see you too. I've missed you." She let her go and stepped back, "Let's see, you went back to your natural hair color," pulling at the ends playfully, "except for the green tips. I like it."

"And I got a new piercing," sticking out her tongue, "See?"

"Hm, yes, I see. I like the hair much better though."

Leo hobbled up to them. "Yes, though why she feels the need to accessorize herself to that extent, I'll never know. You have more metal on you than you weigh. Touching Maggie's cheek gently, "You have such a pretty face. Doesn't she Brenawyn?"

"Of course she does, Nana. Hey, since we have a few minutes before we have to leave for the doctor, Maggie, why don't you show me the new merchandise? I haven't asked Nana about it yet. I'm dying to see it." Brenawyn hooked Maggie's arm and dragged her away into the depths of the store.

Leo's bones may have been brittle, but her ears worked just fine. She smiled as before they moved out of earshot she heard, "You know she doesn't mean anything by that, right?"

Leo busied herself with adjusting the placement of candles and housewares on the shelves nearest the door when Brenawyn called, "Nana, I'm going to run up and take Spencer out for a quick walk, and then I'll be ready to take you to the doctor. Are you all ready?"

"I will be by the time you come back." Hearing the retreating footsteps on the stairs, and then the quickened patter of dog paws on the floor upstairs, Leo put the duster behind the counter and asked Maggie to run upstairs to retrieve her purse from the kitchen counter. By the time Maggie had returned, Leo had her crutches by the front door, waiting for Brenawyn. "You'll be okay while I'm gone, Maggie?"

"I'll have given all the merchandise to wandering strangers before you get back," Maggie rolled her eyes with exaggeration and quickly added, "No problem. Of course I will," before Leo's lips shriveled like a prune in response to her sarcasm.

By the time Brenawyn laid the crutches on the backseat and slid behind the steering wheel, Leo was seat-belted in and fingering the claw marks on the dashboard. "What happened?"

"Oh, I had a bit of a problem with the dog on the way here; seemed he didn't like people walking so close to the car while I was in the bathroom."

"He's never been destructive before. I wonder what got into him. Do you think he'll be okay in the house all by himself?"

"He'll be fine. He's back to his old goofy self now."

~ ~ ~

At the doctor's office, Leo held up her foot and grimaced; "Now it hurts more. They always seem to want you to put your body in a way it doesn't to want to bend," she said as she rubbed her foot.

"We'll know more when the doctor's looked at the films." Brenawyn answered, just as the doctor walked in carrying the x-rays. He smiled as he clipped them to the light box mounted on the opposite wall. "Hello, Mrs. Callahan. I'm Dr. Miller." Leo accepted his extended hand and he turned to face Brenawyn, "And you are?"

"I'm her granddaughter, Brenawyn McAllister."

Looking from one woman to the other, he said, "Ah, I see the resemblance," then quickly got down to business. "All right, let's see what we have."

He turned the overhead lights off and the light box on simultaneously. He contemplated the three x-rays one at a time and made notes in Leo's file. He took two steps to the examining table and, paying careful attention to her injured foot, placed it on the leg rest. He guided Leo to lie flat and slowly took off the air cast she wore. Brenawyn could see that the ankle and foot were badly swollen and bruised.

"You have broken the third, fourth, and fifth metatarsals. They are, luckily, clean breaks and will heal on their own. What has me concerned is the heel; there's a hairline fracture, and if not healed correctly, it will cause pain for the rest of your life."

"What are you going to do?" Leo asked.

Turning on the overhead lights, Dr. Miller answered, "I'm going to have to put a cast on your foot. I am erring on the side of caution; the foot cannot move for fear of aggravating the fracture. That means you will have to stay off your foot for the majority of the day and sleep with it elevated at night. In six to eight weeks, the cast can come off, to be replaced by a removable boot, much like the one you have here," he ended, holding up the hospital-issued air cast.

"Okay, what about stairs? She has stairs at home." Brenawyn asked for clarification.

Leo's head snapped up to the doctor's face and she watched attentively as he responded, "As long as she doesn't overexert herself," he told Brenawyn, and facing Leo to make sure she was listening, he added, "and by that I mean, Mrs. Callahan, you cannot traipse up and down the stairs all day. No more than twice in twenty-four hours. Come down in the morning and then go back up in the evening when ready for bed. And I want you to keep the foot elevated as much as you can throughout the day. Is that clear?"

"Yes, it is. Thank you, doctor."

A half-hour later, Leo was wheeled into the waiting room, sporting a knee-high cast on her right leg.

"Brenawyn,   I   want   to   go   home."

CHAPTER 5

Alex liked walking into The Rising Moon on an ordinary day. He liked the dichotomy of the commercial quartz stone necklaces and love and fortune spell books juxtaposed against the beeswax candles and the sage and lavender bundles lovingly made by the proprietress. There was an authenticity to the shop, once one moved beyond the first two aisles. It was well-masked, and to the untrained eye, it fit in with the dozens of other shops within the city limits, but the walls resonated power which had nothing to do with the location.

Today when he walked in, he was instantly pleased with his timing. A pair of long shapely legs and a fine ass belonging to a woman on a step ladder were just inside the entranceway. She was clad in a pair of denim shorts, and a snug black tee shirt emblazoned with the shop's logo showed off the rest of her figure well. Her ebony hair hid most of her face, but he glimpsed the rosy cheeks and pert nose of Brenawyn, as she glanced over her shoulder. "I'll be right with you. Just let me get this box down." She said as she struggled with the box.

Stepping forward, "Do ye need help?" Alex asked.

"No, it's not heavy. It's just a bit… awkward," she huffed out as she renewed her efforts to wrestle the box off the shelf. "Take a look around and be sure to let me know if you see anything you like."

Alex smiled at her comment and decided to keep his thoughts to himself. She would find them sexist and chauvinistic—not complimentary as he intended them.

He glanced around but his attention was almost immediately brought back to her legs as she raising herself on her toes—complimentary indeed. It did luscious things for her and he itched to run his hand up her leg. She gave a little grunt of satisfaction, which was enough to pull him deeper into his fantasy, but to his disappointment, it only meant that she had the box in hand.

"Ahem."

Alex looked toward the source of the noise and was met with a look of disapproval from Maggie, who stood behind the counter. He sauntered over and gave her a wink, but what he saw sobered him immediately. He caught her chin just before she shied away and angled her head to get a better look. The harshness of the fluorescent light cut through the heavy concealer to reveal the shadow of a faint bruise under her right eye.

"Who dae I need ta ha' a conversation with?" as he touched her cheekbone lightly with his thumb.

Maggie bolted upright and broke contact. She cowered back in the confined space leaning down to brush her hair to cover the telltale contusion, whispering, "No one. I...I fell...fell at home."

Alex followed her gaze to Leo, who was approaching. The weight of her hand on his arm refocused his attention, and with a slight panicked shake of her head, she mouthed,

"Don't. She'll worry."

He'd listen, at least until he investigated further. So when Leo hobbled up to join them, he showed no outward sign of concern, but she was no one's fool.

"Something the matter?"

Maggie didn't look her in the face so it was up to Alex to divert Leo's attention. He leaned against the counter and admitted, "Oops, she caught me," hitching a thumb back at Brenawyn, "appreciating beauty. I'm so ashamed."

Maggie attempted to play along but her laugh was stiff and hollow. Leo furrowed her brow, glancing at her, but Maggie didn't give her any answer. With a ragged sigh, Maggie's shoulders relaxed and she unfolded herself from the corner, a ghost of a smile on her lips. She leaned over the counter, poked him in the chest, and said, "What's wrong with you? Behave yourself! You're acting like a teenager. You're a little old for that, aren't you? That's Brenawyn, Leo's granddaughter, for heaven's sake!"

Alex turned around and now that he could see her face, he recognized the family resemblance. She had her grandmother's big expressive eyes and her dark hair, which was twisted up haphazardly and held by two pens. Tendrils fell about her face attractively. He tore his eyes away from her at last and looked back at Leo, "I met yer granddaughter and her dog this morning at th' bakery. I doonae ken why I didna recognize her then, she resembles ye quite strongly."

"Huh, she didn't mention meeting anyone. Well, anyway, she's staying indefinitely, or so she says. She even quit her job and sold the house."

"Really, she didn't tell me that!" Maggie exclaimed as

43

she bolted from behind the counter and skipped around the two of them.

"Child, you didn't give her a chance." Leo called out as Maggie ran past. "That girl never gives anyone a chance to say anything. Always talking, talking, talking."

Alex admired Maggie's youthful exuberance even though he knew that at this moment it was contrived to avoid a very serious matter. He'd look into that later today. His smile deepened when he heard her squeal as she ambushed Brenawyn. Turning back to Leo, he put his hands on the counter, "Well, it was just a few words over coffee."

Assessing Alex's qualifications with the keen eye of a grandmother, Leo mused, "Perhaps she can find someone else and build a life."

Amused and interested that she would even find him suitable for her only grandchild, he asked, "Wha' makes ye say tha' she wants tha'?"

Shrugging her shoulders, Leo guessed, "Hope?" She looked in the direction of her granddaughter and sighed. "She tells me that she wants to move on with her life. Maybe now she can find one."

Her eyes misted with tears and Alex covered her folded hands with his own, giving them a slight squeeze. Trying to lighten the mood, he suggested, "Well, let's see if I can help," then flashing a big smile, "Formally introduce me ta yer granddaughter, Mrs. Callahan."

"You are too handsome for your own good. And you know it." This response made him grin, and he relaxed to put an elbow on the counter.

"Ah, my charm is working." Grabbing her hands, Alex

looked playfully in her eyes, "Unless...tell me noo. Will ye run away with me instead?"

Slipping her hands from his and slapping at the air in front of him, "Tcha." Leo shook her head in exasperation, and raising her voice to be heard above the instrumental music piped through the store's speakers, "Brenawyn, could you please come over here?"

"Sure, Nana. Be right there."

Leo turned to Alex, "Irreverent clod. No respect for your elders," as she fussed with his collar. "Remember, be good."

"I promise—my verra best, charming self," he playfully answered as he stood up to his full height of 6'5 with blatant exaggeration.

Brenawyn came over, put the box on the counter, and wiped her hands on the back of her denim shorts. "These are the beeswax candles. Are they the ones for the ritual?"

"Yes, they are. Thank you for getting them for me." Drawing Brenawyn's attention to the man standing next to her, Leo made the introductions. "Brenawyn, this is Alexander Sinclair. Alex, this is my granddaughter, Brenawyn McAllister. I believe you two have already met."

She had a strong handshake, confident and self-assured, contradictory to the dainty appearance of her tiny hand in his much larger one. She glanced away, letting her long lashes fall against her rose-kissed cheeks.

"Well, I didna ha' ta wait long ta see ye again."

She smiled genuinely but didn't meet his eyes, "Nana, I met Alex this morning over coffee across the street at the bakery."

"Yes, I know, he told me. He's the one that works at the community college that I told you about this morning."

"Hmm, talking about me already, Leo? Yer granddaughter hasna even fully settled in yet, though I cannae say tha' I'm disappointed," Alex said smugly.

"Away with you and your teasing! I merely mentioned you in case Brenawyn wants to apply for a teaching position at the school. I thought perhaps you could forward her resumé."

More serious now, Alex turned his full attention to Brenawyn. "I could dae tha' for ye if ye wish. Wha' dae ye teach?"

"I taught English literature and composition for seven years, but I'm taking a break from it for the time being to help Nana with the store, especially now that she's in a cast. Of course that is if she can ever be convinced to stop micromanaging and allow me to pick up the slack."

Alex peered over the counter to look at the aforementioned cast and shook his head. "Does this ha' anything ta dae with th' kerfuffle?" Confirmation of his question was reflected in Leo's face. "I think she has ye, woman. Ye cannae participate wi' a cast on yer foot. Gi' o'er ta Brenawyn. Ye have two weeks, more than enough time ta rehearse it with her."

"All right, fine. You got it, and you've seen me do this for years. There's nothing to it. I'll make a list of the items you'll need for the program," Leo added helpfully and hobbled back to the office, leaving Brenawyn and Alex standing at the counter staring at each other. Brenawyn made a face, and Alex realized she was looking over his shoulder. He turned to find Maggie rearranging a shelf to no purpose close by, whistling in tune with the Celtic music that was playing on the sound system. Looking back, Brenawyn's face was now devoid of emotion, whatever had passed between them was undecipherable to him.

"So, what can I help you with today, Alex?"

"Leo called me yesterday morn and told me tha' two books tha' I ordered finally arrived."

"Hmm, let's see," she circled the counter and after a short search found a pile of ordered items waiting to be picked up. She squatted down to rummage through it. "So, you're a teacher at the community college? What do you teach?"

"I'm an anthropology professor but I also teach a class on Celtic lore and mythology." He answered, looking over the counter at her.

Brenawyn found the books and handed them to him. She stood up to find Alex digging in his back pocket for his wallet. "How much dae I owe ye?"

Brenawyn crossed to the register and rang up the sale, "The total is $56.79. That's interesting, anthropology and mythology. I bet you're a great storyteller." She stopped and looked away, the blush creeping back up her neck, but then continued. "Especially with your accent. Where are you from?"

"Yes, I ha' been told tha'." He leaned on the counter. "If ye ever have an evening to spare, I could tell ye one or…" he moved closer to her, "two."

Brenawyn let out a giggle. "Well, I might have taken you up on that, but something tells me I'd be getting more than a story."

Smiling, he handed his credit card to Brenawyn. "Yer loss, then. As to whaur I call home, Scotland, a wee place near Roslyn, around sixteen kilometers from Edinburgh."

Her quest to complete the transaction came to a halt when she couldn't locate a pen. She looked on the shelves underneath the register and on the floor, coming up to ask him to wait until she retrieved one from the back.

"May I?" Alex asked, reaching over. A puzzled look washed over her face. Her mouth opening slightly, to voice a protest perhaps, but nothing came out. She leaned closer.

He reached behind her and pulled out the scissored pens holding her hair. Waves of raven hair fell about her shoulders, and she smoothed the errant strands away from her face. "Ye should leave yer hair doon. 'Tis beautiful." He reverently reached for a wayward tendril with a knuckle and gently tucked it behind her ear.

"Um. Thank you. I appreciate that." Brenawyn blushed again.

Alex signed the receipt and looked at the clock on the wall behind her, then verified the time with his own watch. "Och, I ha' ta go, but I will see ye again."

"Oh?"

"Aye, ye may have just volunteered for this thing on Thursday next, but many o' us were corralled and beaten inta submission by yer wee grandmother in thaur." he admitted, gesturing to the back room.

A mysterious sparkle in his eye had Brenawyn changing postures. Coming out from behind the counter, she took the time to slowly look him over with a playful half-smile on her lips, "Beaten into submission is it? And here I was thinking that you were a strong, braw lad, well capable to fending off the sting of a small woman." Brenawyn leaned back on the counter and crossed her arms, "Tsk. Too bad."

Alex registered her deliberate perusal and broke out in laughter. "Ah aye, I see wha's happening haur. Ye've decided ta flirt with th' master. Verra guid." He spread his arms wide and took a few steps backward. "Ta th' victor go th' spoils."

As he exited the store, he shared a look with Maggie, who hovered by the door. Knowing she'd find an excuse to follow him out, he stopped in front of the window of the next shop. He heard the faint chime of the Rising Moon's door and turned in time to meet her. Her eyes were brimming with tears, "Please, Alex. Don't do anything. It was my fault... I made him mad."

"Maggie, was it yer jakey knob, Buchanan?"

"Please..."

"Margaret, ye doonae ha' to be afeart. I'll take care o' him."

CHAPTER 6

Brenawyn looked over the list her grandmother had made last night and counted two things that were actually specified—the candles, which she had retrieved from the shelf yesterday, and the ceremonial robes, which she knew were boxed in the office closet. She went into the office and located the robes which were, surprisingly, hung up and pressed in a garment bag. Every year, she would take these full length robes out for her grandmother, luxuriating in the cool, smooth feel of the white and green silk. Emerald and silver embroidery in a Celtic knot design decorated the lapels, back placket, and the cuffs of the wide bell sleeves. The sleeves were further lined with an emerald silk dyed to match the embroidery. The bottom eighteen inches of the white silk was vertically cut every six inches and embroidered to reveal six inches of the green, cut in a similar fashion. It was the most beautiful garment that she had ever seen.

Brenawyn didn't hear her grandmother approach, absorbed as she was. Leo hobbled into the room and joined her at the closet to admire the robe. "It's an antique, you know. I never knew whether to believe the provenance, but I bought it from a woman who told me quite a story about it. In the back of my mind, the place that no reality or logic resides, I want it to be true because it's romantic," Leo mused.

Drawn out of her ruminations and interested by the promise of a romantic story, Brenawyn turned. "I can't believe you never told me this one. Here, sit down and I'll pull up a chair. Tell me everything. You know I love this stuff. Wait, first, do you need anything?"

"No, honey I'm fine," Leo answered as she carefully sat down in the office chair.

Considering whether her grandmother needed anything she wouldn't ask for, and deciding the answer was no, Brenawyn settled down in the chair opposite the desk, "Ok, spill," she urged.

"Let's see. I bought the robe back, hmm, over thirty-five years ago, well before I had this place. I bought it from a woman named Rosalyn Feegan when I went to Ireland with your grandfather. We had been on an extended vacation, staying with his family and mine alternately. During the first week I wandered into a shop and I bought a few items of no consequence. Weeks later, I found myself back at the same shop on one of my many solitary walks to escape the family bickering. Rosalyn was the owner, and we got to talking. I thought she was odd, more than odd, the way I would catch her looking at me periodically, like she expected some great surprise at any moment. It really was strange. But she was a fantastic storyteller, and before long I was caught up in her tales, eager for another when she had finished the last."

"Sounds interesting," Brenawyn agreed.

"It was. She told me the legends. I had heard them all

before, but the way she told them, it was like she had been there. She made it believable, that if I walked out and over the next hill I would be carried off by the Faerie themselves. So at last, she tells me that she has something for me and she takes me in the back of the store and thrusts this robe into my arms, blathering on about waiting so long for the next guardian."

Brenawyn made a face, "What?"

"Well, I guess you had to be there. So, she takes me out to the front again, and switches the sign that was hanging on the front door to 'closed.' Then she tells me, hushed-like, that it is the ceremonial robe of the last Druid high priestess."

Laughter bubbled out of Brenawyn's throat, as she looked at the robe behind her grandmother, "That's a fancy story. You should let the reporters that cover the event tomorrow have that story. The tourists would love it."

"Well, no, I've never been tempted to tell anyone until now, but that's not the end of it, though. Rosalyn waited for some reaction from me, but she looked confused that I didn't give her one."

"Good story, Nana." Brenawyn said.

"Oh, I'm not done. There's more. I guess because Lughnasadh is just a few days away, it has put what she said in my mind. Well, according to the story, on Beltane, after the rituals had been performed and the eternal fire relit, the high priestess and the Shaman of the Order would humm mmm. You know."

"What? You mean have sex?" Brenawyn asked astonished. "I thought that only a part of the King Arthur legend. Though, if my memory serves, it was the high priestess and the King of England that did the deed."

"Uh huh, to ensure the continued fruitfulness of the nation. Yes, where do you think the authors got the idea? Only in their literary vision it was more dramatic to have it be the King for the superstitious blessing for the continued health and wealth of the nation instead of two devoted followers of a religion to ensure the continuation of their dogma."

"Wow, you were right, though. It is barbaric and yet… um, romantic is the word, I guess, to have two people so devoted, if not to each other, but to a similar cause."

Glancing at the robe with new interest, Brenawyn turned to leave, then remembered, "Oh Nana, I have a few questions about the rest of this list." Unfolding the list from her back pocket Brenawyn approached her grandmother. "What specific stones do I need for each of the positions in the circle?"

"Oh, that's up to you. The stones used are unique to each person that casts. Go out and pick any five that appeal to you," shooing her out the door. "Go take them off the shelves."

"How will I know if I pick the right ones?"

"Dear, whichever you pick will be the correct stones for you."

With that, Brenawyn exited the office and walked into the showroom of the store. She first stopped at the sectioned bin piled with a variety of polished stones. She loved to touch them; many felt warm, as if alive, while others were cold. Running her hands across each, she closed her eyes, but hadn't a clue as to which ones to pick. She walked toward the case against the far wall that housed the larger stones and geodes; each was displayed with a card listing their properties, with variations of cleansing and balancing energies on each marker. She knew instinctively that the descriptions would do her no good. She opened the cabinet, feeling drawn to touch them. She handled each in a reverent way, but discarded most immediately, placing them back with care. Others she placed on the velvet covered countertop, unsure as to her final choices. She narrowed it down to seven, and stood back and considered them.

Reaching for the amethyst first, she ran her fingers along the smooth edges, mesmerized by the crystals within. She placed it as the first in a new configuration at the top of the velvet mat, knowing in her mind that she would pair it with air. She then turned to place the blue tourmaline with water on the left, bloodstone with earth on the right, obsidian with fire towards the bottom, and finally placing the tiger's eye with spirit in the center of the mat.

She was startled when her grandmother gasped behind her. Turning around, she noted Leo staring at the stones. "What's the matter?"

Leo shook her head mutely.

"What? You're worrying me. What's the matter?" Brenawyn ran to her side but Leo brushed her off and stumbled toward the counter.

"These stones. Why did you pick these stones? And why did you arrange them in this way?"

"Nana, calm down. You're scaring me. You told me to pick any stones that I wanted, right? These just felt right.

The amethyst, I think would be obvious, it's my birthstone. The tiger's eye—I remember Grandpa having a tie tack with a tiger's eye stone. Do you remember?"

"Yes, I do." Leo said hesitantly.

"Wasn't he buried with it?

"Yes, he was."

"All right then, the blue tourmaline and obsidian—I liked the colors, they are soothing. The blue is calming, and the black is so deep, I just find myself wanting to touch it, to stroke its smoothness. And then last, bloodstone. I guess it's my way of tipping a hat to the pagan in this endeavor." Brenawyn finished. "So now, do you want to tell me what this is all about?" Brenawyn asked as she abandoned the stones on the counter and pulled Leo away.

Leo looked back and shook her head slowly with the echo of fear in her eyes.

"All right, this is not funny. Tell me."

"It's nothing," Leo replied unconvincingly. "It's probably nothing," she grabbed Brenawyn's chin and gently forced it down so she could look into her eyes. "Maggie, can you mind the store," she called.

Maggie responded, "Sure thing, Leo. B, do you want me to wrap these up and put them with the other things to go down to the park while you're—

"No leave them there," Leo interrupted, splaying her hand on the center tiger's eye. Leave them exactly how they are right now."

"Ok. You're the boss," Maggie meekly replied. Confused at the sudden mood change, she looked at Brenawyn to get a hint at the cause, but seeing no answer registered in her face, she turned to resume her inventory.

"We will be upstairs awhile. Do not disturb us."

Upstairs, Leo told Brenawyn to sit at the kitchen table and wait while she haltingly went into her bedroom and pulled a brown storage box from under her bed. Fumbling with the plastic latch, she opened it to reveal her daughter, Margaret's, belongings. She found the journal she sought and went to join Brenawyn in the pantry.

Brenawyn eyed the journal Leo put on the counter but didn't say a word. Leo glanced at her granddaughter, knowing that she was expecting an explanation, and from the slight smile on her face probably thought Leo had finally lost her mind.

She took a fortifying breath and began, "The reason for my reaction to your choice is that I used those stones in that configuration, that exact configuration, many years ago—twenty-nine years to be exact." stressing the last part of the declaration. Pausing for any sign of recognition but receiving none, she asked, "Had your mother told you anything about it?"

"Nana, what's all of this about? I told you I chose the stones because I thought they were pretty. What does this have to do with something that happened before I was born? And why would my mother, of all people, tell me about it?"

"I didn't think she did, but I had to make sure. Your mother wouldn't have told you because your father ardently opposed her religion, and your mother loved him. So she abandoned the beliefs in which she was raised to be with him. Then she was pregnant and she found out how far she would go to protect the one she loved more than her husband, more than her life." Touching Brenawyn's cheek, "She made the right choice. I would have done the same, even though her actions ruined her marriage."

Sitting up in apparent indignation, Brenawyn did what any good daughter would do, she rushed to the aid of her deceased father, a loving, albeit strict, man.

"Shhh. Wait, don't say anything." Leo interrupted her, "Hear me out, then you can scream and rant and tell me to go the devil, but you must listen to me. I have kept the secret for too long because your mother begged me to as long as your father was alive. Then after he died, I didn't know how to tell you."

Through tight lips, Brenawyn mumbled, "Go on," as she turned away from Leo a bit. She crossed her arms tightly over her chest and looked at the wall of cabinets.

"Your mother met your father when she just turned nineteen and he was twenty-four. He was handsome and charming and swept your mother off her feet. Their relationship and courting was tumultuous. She would be in high spirits, humming and singing, dancing with Grandpa in the kitchen and then she would be depressed and weeping. She'd lie in bed until late morning and drag through the day. We tried to talk to her about her relationship, but she refused to listen. She wouldn't confide in either of us about what troubled her. She was secretive. Then one day, she ran off to get married. It broke our hearts, Grandpa's especially.

"They returned, and after our shock faded, we found out the reason for her mood swings. Brian was a fundamentalist and would not tolerate any other belief in his household. Later, he wouldn't tolerate even us for our beliefs, even though Margaret had renounced them. It was a strain on our relationship. Seeing us even for an afternoon was enough to cause vicious arguments that lasted days. The strain, I guess, became too much to bear and they moved away." Leo paused to sniff and wipe her eyes.

Brenawyn turned in her chair to face her. Having been deprived of her mother at nine, Leo knew she had only vague memories—a fragment of a song her mother used to sing at bedtime and the scent of her perfume. The rest, over time, had blurred.

Leo had mixed feelings about giving Brenawyn something tangible of Margaret's to hold onto. What would Brenawyn think of her when she told her that she'd held onto her mother's journals? Kept them from her? Would she understand? No, not yet, and perhaps she never would.

"She was pregnant with you when Grandpa died. Somehow, she talked Brian into letting her come to stay with me for a month by herself. She insisted that we stay at the farm, shunning anything to do with my religious beliefs and the shop, here. We buried Grandpa and she helped me go through his things; it was a relief to have her there. Despite her choice, she was like she always had been—the happy Margaret, humming and singing.

"As the days passed, though, I could see her becoming more introverted. I would catch her daydreaming, I suppose, but with a concentrated look on her face. She told me on the third day after that she couldn't feel you move anymore. At first, she told, me she thought that it was normal, but after the third day, she was sure that something was wrong. She was seven months along and three days of little movement.

Yes, we both thought something was wrong.

"I asked if she wanted me to call Brian, but she was emphatically opposed to calling him. She said she didn't want to worry him if it turned out to be nothing. So we made an appointment at my gynecologist, who at the time still delivered babies. Now he's dead, of course," Leo added as an aside.

"Wait, of course everything turned out fine. I'm here. Am I not?

"Yes," kissing her forehead then giving a small sad smile, "and thank the powers that be for that." She reached to get the journal she had brought and handed it to Brenawyn. "I think you should read this. This is one of your mother's journals, the first that she wrote. It will do a better job at explaining what happened."

"My mother wrote? How come I never knew that?" Not wanting or needing an answer yet, Brenawyn looked at the plain blue cloth-covered journal and sighed with happiness as she hugged the book to her chest.

"Margaret started writing at that time, and for years after, sending the completed journals to me when she filled them. There are three. She seemed intent on putting it all on paper to document it, in case...you ever wanted to know."

Puzzled, Brenawyn nodded her head, but she wasn't listening to Leo any longer. She was more concerned with the fact that she had three whole journals of her mother's writing to read.

Pushing the book on her again, "Read it and I'll give you the others. After..." Stopping to look around, Leo hobbled out to the living room to return with the bouquet of flowers that had seen too many days, "I have to show you something first. Hmm, I'm glad I didn't throw these flowers out yet. They will serve as a good demonstration," Leo said.

"What did she feel was so important? Not that I'm complaining, but I'm a little scared by the way you're telling me this."

"Hush and pay attention to the flowers. Then you can read it." Leo closed her eyes and concentrated. "Blessed Ones, make me your vessel so I may bring about healing the Earth. Let the healing of the Waters run through me as I do your biding."

Mesmerized by her grandmother's words, Brenawyn's eyes drifted to her instead of the flowers as she had been instructed. Her grandmother was relaxed as she said the words, obviously expecting something to happen just as Brenawyn knew nothing would.

Brenawyn made a small sharp movement and let out a soft cry as, in exaggerated slowness, an iridescent blue pattern began to glow under her grandmother's skin as she reached out to touch the flowers. The leached, muted colors of the petals turned more vibrant and the stem regained its rigidity. Turning back time, the flowers no longer wilted, and they gained the freshness of the newly picked.

Brenawyn found herself on her feet next to her grandmother though she hadn't remembered getting up out of the chair. She reached down to lightly touch the still glowing runes on her grandmother's arm. "What. Are. These?" Taking the hand and extending the arm, she saw that the runes covered it from finger tips to shoulder and beyond as the gape in the blouse's armhole revealed.

Leo turned to her granddaughter and purposely opened her eyes. Gone were her soft green eyes, replaced by iridescent irises matching the runes. "Look at the flowers, Brenawyn. It's important that you know. My beliefs are real. They are ancient and they are strong after all these years. You had to see this before you read the journal because it will give validity to what's in it."

"What did you... how did you...?" then finally giving up on formulating a coherent question, asked the more important one, "What are you?"

Laughing, Leo responded, "I'm a Druid, Brenawyn."

CHAPTER 7

January 31, 1986

My Sweet Girl,
I thought I knew what love was. Not bothering to listen to my parents—your grandparents—when they ranted and pleaded with me to give my relationship more time. They were wrong. They didn't understand that I love your father, but at the same time, they were right about me not knowing what love actually was. Until I found out that I was pregnant I didn't know to what lengths a mother would go to protect her child: beg, borrow, steal, trade her life, or sell her soul. I didn't know what lengths I would travel to protect my child until it was upon me and the child yet unborn. Now, I know.

I went to stay with your grandmother after my father's death, and shortly thereafter I broke down and asked her to take me to her doctor after three days of not feeling you move much. I also asked her not to call your father, because I didn't want to worry him unnecessarily; but truth be told, I wanted time to keep my options open.

Sent home with a prescription for bed rest and pregnancy hormones in a last ditch effort to try to save you, I knew this was only done to ease my mind and help me begin to accept the inevitable. By the time we had arrived back home, my mind was made up. I asked your grandmother to help.

Looking back, this was the point that my life's focus changed. I made several decisions at that moment that had nothing to do with the man I had married and the consequences that I knew would ruin what we had. Once Brian was the center of my universe, now you were.

Your father is a devout fundamentalist, as you probably know. But what you may not know is that he is, was, intolerant of all other belief systems. I'm sorry. This is hard. The husband I know and the father you will come to know may be two different people. I hope that is the case, but somehow… I doubt it.

The man I know, he didn't accept that I had a very different religious background and asked me not only to convert but spurn it after we married. Please don't hate me. If he knew that there was something wrong with you, he'd be convinced that if the baby died—if you died—it was the will of God.

I asked my mother to perform a protection spell for you. I had seen her perform this ritual many times, and while it wasn't a surefire way of holding onto the pregnancy, I hoped that it would shift it more into the realm of possibility. She didn't respond at first, taking me up and depositing me in her bed; but minutes later, I heard the noise as she tore apart her stillroom looking for the ingredients.

She reappeared with a basket brimming with things she'd need. She took out her grimoire, the page of the protection spell dog-eared, and she ran through the list of ingredients to be sure she hadn't forgotten anything. She took out her mortar and pestle and began by grinding pine needles—the smell wafted through the room almost instantly.

As Leo muttered under her breath, I saw the telltale sign of the working of a spell; the iridescent runes glowing brightly under her skin. She set up candles at six points in the room, four at exact compass points. The fifth, she climbed precariously on the bed to put in the hanging candelabra above the it for spirit, and the last one she made me hold for body.

She put the ground pine needles at the bottom of the bed in the pestle and tied a sprig of lavender to the brass headboard. She kissed my cheek then, and began chanting in earnest. She lit the candles, called the Spirits, and then laid small stones on my stomach individually. I remember the meaning behind her choice of stones because she declared them in her chant, though I cannot remember all the words. The first was amethyst—to transform my pain into healing, the next, bloodstone—to instill courage. Blue tourmaline was the third, placed to help connect the body and mind to allow faith to heal me physically. The fourth stone was obsidian. Working in harmony with the tourmaline it would grant access to the strength of my faith to heal me. Specific to the reproductive system, tiger's eye was chosen as the fifth stone to provide balance and strength to get through the process.

I must have made some sort of protest when the dagger appeared and my mother sliced her palm and then reached for my hand with her bloodied one. She looked at me abruptly, stopping the chant for a few beats and ruthlessly grabbed my arm. She sliced my palm, ignored my hiss of pain, then grabbed the hand with her own and forcefully squeezed the open wounds together so the blood mingled as it fell upon the sixth candle in my other hand.

Her tone changed markedly and became quiet. In direct opposition, the stones became warm, unnaturally warm; but I did not struggle as my mother guided my hands to cradle my growing child, and placed her own on the top of my belly.

With the last words of the incantation, it was as if the air and energy of the room expended itself in one burst of light and heat concentrated on the crystals. The crystals grew painfully bright, and I gasped for air several times, allowing a great whoosh of air into my lungs, and then all five stones burst into fine shimmering powder that was absorbed into my exposed skin.

Moving in slow motion, I tried wiping it from my skin, only to think bemusedly how pretty it looked glinting in the fading light of the room. I looked at my mother for explanation but she stared stupidly at me and crumbled to the floor. Panic-stricken now, I slid to the floor beside her but an intense gripping seized me and I huddled in a ball to wait its end. Groaning and crying out, I thought that this must be what a miscarriage felt like.

Flashes of memory are all I remember. Gentle hands lifting me, cool compresses on my forehead, calming words, fading in and out with long exaggerated spans of silence. I think I dreamed. More words, not so gentle now, crashing things, glass tinkling, gentle hands again. More strange dreams.

I awoke to changes. Gone was my mother's room, replaced by a sterile hospital room, and Brian slumped in the corner chair, asleep. I was bone tired, and I lay back on the bed assessing. I felt tired but energized, lethargic but alive. I felt... you move!

I pulled up my nightgown to look at my belly. I was far enough along that I could see the movement, and I was immediately granted another look at the slow undulation as you resettled. I screamed my elation, and startled Brian. Bleary eyed, he rushed to the bed, not knowing what had roused him. He took a quick assessment of my condition, holding my head between his hands, then my belly, his eyes round at your strong kick, then his arms were around me, crushing me to his chest, crying.

He held me for endless minutes, and then I felt tension creep into his frame. His hands grabbed my upper arms in a vice-like grip, shaking me until my teeth rattled he spit, "You are never to see your mother again. I forbid it!

CHAPTER 8

Her grandmother said she was a Druid. Brenawyn knew this. How many times after she came to live with Leo had she seen things? But magic was supposed to be just trickery and sleight of hand stuff. She had never given it any thought otherwise; it was just cool tricks to occupy a child. But the magic was real? Was she honestly expected to believe that? What explanation was there for the glowing pattern on her grandmother's arms? And the flower thing had astounded her, true. She hadn't seen anything that would betray a trick, so if it were real, if she could make the wilted flowers bloom again… could she have done anything for Liam? Could she have saved him? Could she still? Brenawyn couldn't bear an answer to that question.

Hooking the leash onto Spencer's collar, Brenawyn quietly crept down the stairs, not wanting to face her grandmother yet. Her feelings were in turmoil and she didn't trust herself to speak without saying something irrevocable. The dog, however, was eager to walk, and dragged Brenawyn down the stairs with all the stealth of a herd of elephants. The last thing she heard as she closed the door was her grandmother call, "Brenawyn, honey, do you want to talk?" Despite her heart's pang, she locked the door and turned away without a word in response, her brain insisting on time to think.

The streets were quaintly lit by street lights that resembled gas lamps, and in the near distance she saw candle-led groups on the ghost tour. Laughter floated to her from a nearby late night bistro with café tables still out lining the wide sidewalk. As she walked past, a man looked up admiringly at her only to be chastised by his date for looking at another woman. She hurried along, not interested in being the immediate cause, albeit not the source, of the strangers' argument.

Further down, only a few people dotted the street. She stopped at a window, peering in to look at the antiques and collectibles. Tomorrow she'd return to rummage through the articles in the store. Perhaps she'd see something that caught her eye. Before turning away she caught her reflection in the glass and was startled by it— hair severely pulled back in a ponytail and big eyes staring out of a face that was too pale. She looked like she was in desperate need of sleep, sun, and perhaps some make-up; she reached up to pinch her cheeks. A breeze blew and she shivered. It was unseasonably chilly for summer, even for Massachusetts.

Decision hesitantly made, she walked across the street and headed for home. She passed close to a tour group as they stood in front of the tavern that the witch trial victim, Bridget Bishop, was said to haunt. Brenawyn stopped to hear the tale for a moment, enamored with the telling. When it was done, she flashed a brilliant smile at the tour guide before he protested a non-paying listener. The smile seemed to placate him and he glanced back to look at her several times as he proceeded with his tour.

"Hello, beautiful." A husky masculine voice behind her startled her out of her thoughts. Propelled backward by her dog, pulling on his collar enough to make him choke, she twisted, stumbling into Alex's arms as the dog pranced at their feet. She could feel the blush rush into her cheeks as she realized her breasts were pressed against his chest and her bottom cupped in his hands. She planted both her hands on his chest and pushed off. He held on for a fraction of a second too long before he relinquished her.

"Oh, I'm so sorry," as Brenawyn extricated herself from his embrace and lightly brushed at his shirt. "Are you okay? Did I hurt you?" At his perusal, she was made all too aware of her outfit— a white lacy top and beige shorts which revealed too much of her legs.

"Nay, o' course no'. Think nothing o' it. Are ye on yer way back home?"

"Yes, but just to get a sweater out of my car. I didn't realize the night would be so chilly."

At the mention of the weather, a strong breeze blew, raising gooseflesh on her bare arms, and even in the dim light shed by the street lamp, she knew he could make out the straining of nipples against the soft shirt. Unashamedly staring, he took his time tearing his eyes away and offered his arm, "Would ye like me to accompany ye back ta yer car then?"

"If you're sure that I'm not keeping you from anything," Brenawyn answered, unsure.

"Nothing that willna wait. So how are ye?"

"I'm fine, just out for a walk with the pooch, trying to clear my head."

"Troubled? Having second thoughts about moving haur?"

"No, not that, but trying to…adjust to some new information."

"New information?"

"Yeah, nothing really, just surprising is all." Shaking her head, "It's nothing of import." Blatantly changing topics, Brenawyn asked, "So did you do anything fun after I saw you today?"

Alex laughed, "Well, no' fun. I had ta work. I taught an evening class ta a bunch o' sophomoric individuals who rained infantile questions at me about Beltaine rights, even though Lughnasadh is in a few days. Most o' them will be at th' park ta catch my bit at th' beginning, since someone in th' class found out I was a part o' it."

"And what are you doing for that?" Brenawyn asked, interested and half surprising herself, thrilled that she would be seeing him again so soon.

"I am going ta give some background history on th' ceremony, explaining wha' th' feast celebrates, wha' each part o' th' ceremony means, and its significance, as an introduction ta ye." Rolling his eyes heavenward, "I even ha' a costume tha' I ha' been persuaded ta wear."

She laughed, "Oh, my friend, you will not be alone on that count. I have one too. Though I don't mind wearing it, it's beautiful."

"Ye would make anything bonny."

Brenawyn stopped in front of The Rising Moon and looked up at him, "Thank you. I appreciate the compliment, even though I know that you're exaggerating." Pausing to look at her car, then upstairs, she continued, "If you have time, I'll go and bring the dog upstairs, and we can continue our walk."

Catching her hand, and caressing the back of it, he said, "I'll wait; and Brenawyn, I was no' exaggerating."

Breath hitching in her throat she nodded dumbly at him and turned to unlock the door, trying to calm her hammering heart. "I'll be right back."

Running the dog upstairs, she unhooked his leash, and gently kissed her sleeping grandmother on the cheek. Covering her with the afghan from the couch, Brenawyn's earlier concerns were temporarily forgotten. Spencer sniffed Leo's hand and in her sleep she patted the dog's head. He lay down, giving a doggie grunt as he settled himself at the base of the couch.

Brenawyn pulled at her restrained hair, quickly ran a brush through it, and grabbed a sweater from her room. She paused at the open door, looking back at Leo, and quietly whispered to her sleeping grandmother, "I'm not mad. I just have to digest it for a while. We will talk, but I'm not ready yet. I love you."

Locking the door behind her, she wasn't quite prepared for Alex leaning against her car. He was the picture of masculinity and sex, with rippling biceps and well-muscled thighs in form-fitting blue jeans that left little to the imagination. A full head of dark wavy hair fell to brush the collar of his shirt, too long to be professional, and a day or two's growth of beard. Her mouth went dry with the thought of how it would feel against her skin. He smelled good too, of soap and sun and mmm… man, remembering in vivid detail her short stay in his arms. He gave her a sexy smile, noting her perusal. *Pull yourself together and stop staring like you want to have him for dessert.*

"Are ye sure ye're going ta be warm enough in tha'?" nodding to her sweater.

"I'll be fine as long as we keep walking." Stepping down off the stairs, she took his hand and they began walking. "So, what stories did the students beg you to tell them?"

Alex looked sideways at her, "Are ye sure ye want ta hear tha'?"

"Yes, I love mythology, and it's filled with risqué stories about the gods and goddesses. You'll find that I am a rapt audience and won't laugh and titter about every little innuendo."

"Och, then it will truly be a change o' pace. Just based on test scores, I think everyone is thaur ta hear those stories; no one listens ta me otherwise," he responded, laughing at himself.

"Oh wait, you didn't tell me that there would be an exam. Damn, let me think…" chiding him and stepping playfully closer so her hip and the length of her leg brushed him. "No, I still want to hear."

"Aaricht, but I did warn ye." Alex began, "Wait until we get to the park. The town finished setting up for th' ceremony. It will be a good backdrop for auld stories."

"Setting a mood, are you?"

"Wha' storyteller doesna?" Squeezing her hand, he said, "Besides, I think ye'll like it."

They walked in companionable silence until the park

came into view. "Haur we are." He stood back to let her take it in.

Standing at the edge of the grassy park in the center of town, Brenawyn looked around and thought that the architect of the park had some forethought, with oaks and sycamores planted at intervals surrounding the grassy knoll. Stopping mid-step she whistled low and quipped, "Jeez, the residents do not take the tourist lure lightly here."

At the center, new to the park's landscape, standing stones stood as silent sentinels awaiting some ancient and sacred ritual. Come daylight, she suspected the surrounding backdrop complete with cars, buses, museum-style velvet ropes, and quaint stands selling the usual variety of souvenirs wouldn't be enough to diminish the pull of the circle.

"Aye, tha' is th' truth o' it." Alex responded. "Though thaur are quite a few people haur tha' are believers in Druidism and Wicca, 'tis mainly in th' observance o' th' high feasts: Beltane, Lughnasadh, Samhain, and Oimelc.

Brenawyn approached and held out a tentative hand to the nearest stone to assure herself that it was real. She turned to Alex, who trailed behind her, and asked, "They're so beautiful," running her hand along a vein, "Where did they come from?"

"Since th' town has reclaimed its ugly history, they ha' spared nay expense at cashing in on th' commercialism. They were imported from Ireland—solid slabs o' blue stone from th' same deposit." Indicating with his arm, "Look, ye can see th' similarities in th' stones."

Brenawyn walked slowly around the interior of the

circle, half day-dreaming, thinking about her grandmother and the wild implications of her story. Then turning back, "Alex, do you know anything about these circles? What were they used for?"

"Ceremonies, rituals, some say sacrifice, but they were built on points of power. Beyond th' cutting and transport of th' stones, thaur was geometry, astronomy, and astrology ta be considered afore th' placement. Most circles are oriented with th' rising and the setting of the sun, though only at certain times of th' year does the sun align with th' stones in perfect harmony. Next week is one. This one haur is oriented in such a way, but th' effect is lost because civilization blocks th' true vista of dawn and dusk."

Pausing for a moment, Alex then continued, "Druidism is a nature-based religion. All ceremonies revolve around healing and protection. Spells—that's a topic for another time, but generally, afore any ceremony th' celebrant would go out th' night afore or th' morning o' th' ceremony and perform a private rite ta ask permission o' th' Earth ta cast on its ground." Alex let go of her hand and stepped back.

Brenawyn looked up from inspecting the nearest stone, interest piqued, and asked, "Really, why do you think that was?"

"It was because," he said, "th' Earth and everything tha' sprang from it were held sacred by th' Druids. Th' Earth is a live entity, and ta cast without permission was disrespectful."

He walked around the center offertory pedestal, "Though thaur were, and still are, male Druids, usually th' celebrants were women." Looking back at Brenawyn to placate any question that she might have, "It may have had something ta dae with women's ability ta bear children, th' fertility of th' woman symbolically representing th' fertility o' th' Earth. The celebrant would cleanse herself ta wash away impurities and don a blessed garment with th' help o' her attendants, then prepare and perform th' ceremony, fulfilling all th' requirements for it. Then as an offering on specific holy days such as Beltane, th' celebrant would willingly offer herself as a symbol of fertility."

"Offered herself to anyone?"

"Tha' was rarely th' case, though at times it happened. It usually was th' Shaman of the Order. The high priestess and the shaman were th' two responsible for perpetuation o' th' beliefs. He was ta retain and protect all knowledge of th' Order. Her responsibility was by far th' weightier. She communed with nature and th' spirits through ritual."

"What of children that came about through these…um… liaisons?"

"Ah, sex was seen differently then. Any child tha' was conceived from such a union led a blessed life. They were seen as nature's blessing, and therefore received th' adoration o' th' Druids."

"What story did you tell your students in class today?"

"Aye, I did promise ye a tale." Alex nodded and paced toward the nearest standing stone. He touched it and looked back at Brenawyn. "A while sin[2] this world was th' home o' th' Celtic gods, but they decided ta retreat ta th' realm o' Tir-Na-Nog when faith was no' enough for man anymore.

---

[2] Some time ago

Immortals all, they felt th' loss o' having mortal beings so close tha' many o' them would visit this realm ta be in th' company of such radiance. Ye ken, mortal life gives off a vibrant aura. Watching them fight environmental conditions, illness, and starvation, and celebrate life and unions ta make their mark, made th' gods envious. Their observations became interactions as they tried ta understand th' mortals need ta be. In their search, they found tha' mortals had emotion more profound than any god had experienced. They found through these interactions tha' th' vistas were more beautiful, food tasted sweeter, and th' cries o' their lovers were more arousing.

"Cernunnos, th' god o' th' hunt, craved mortal com-panionship. He would disguise himself as a stag and move amongst th' forest glades whaur a crystal clear stream flowed. Time and again, he would watch as women would come ta th' stream ta collect water. For many moons, he would stand in th' brush and just observe. Ta any who cared ta look, a stag would be all they would see.

"After a time, he grew tired o' this and yearned for a closer connection ta th' gaily dressed, laughing women who traveled together, sometimes ta get water, rarely ta bathe. These times were most desirous, for th' obvious reasons, and one tha' made him th' most curious. Th' women, after they had washed th' dirt from their bodies, would relax with an easy companionship, moments he guessed were few and far between. Th' episodes would always end too early, and he craved more.

"One day he got up enough courage ta step out of th' thick underbrush as one single woman with auburn hair curling down ta her waist was bending ta get a bucketful o' water. Bright copper and silver shone as th' dappled sunlight fell on her glorious mane, paling th' verdant surroundings. He longed ta touch it. She gasped when she saw him, an enormous twelve point buck, just on th' other side o' th' stream.

"Water sloshed from th' bucket as she picked it up with shaky hands ta place on th' ground next ta her. She smoothed her damp skirts and tried to remain still, lowering her eyes ta th' ground as she was taught. She was scared, more afraid than she ever had been, and when th' buck stepped inta the water, she trembled.

"She risked a glance at its face after th' initial shock wore off. Cernunnos stood thaur, falling in love with the brash sense of adventure tha' made her leuk at him despite her childhood lessons. He was roused at th' quick pulse at her throat, and th' thought tha' he alone could make it race.

"He let her go, interested as she turned time and again ta catch another glimpse o' him as she traipsed back ta her village.

"He returned on th' next full moon and she was thaur waiting. When he approached softly, she held out a tentative hand. As she brushed th' fur on his neck with her fingertips, he sighed, amazed ta find th' stories had been true. Th' touch o' a mortal was like nay other. He leaned inta her hand ta get more. Emboldened, she buried her hands in his soft fur, whispering soft endearments and prayers ta th' gods for showing their favor.

"Each full moon they met and he carried her ta vistas so beautiful, in this world and Tir-Na-Nog, as ta make her weep. She lay close ta his side as she watched waterfalls, sunsets, or th' waves crashing on th' shore o' a remote beach. Once, she nuzzled close and whispered words o' love into his neck.

"Cernunnos heard this, but until then had nay idea wha' th' feeling building in him was. His heart rejoiced, and he shifted inta his godly form, th' form o' man, but unlike any man kent ta earth. Cernunnos is th' horned god, so while a man, magnificent in form, he had th' antlers o' th' buck, shortened as a sign o' his office and duty.

"She shifted ta give him freedom o' movement, but when she eased back ta lounging, it was inta th' arms o' Cernunnos. He held her tight as th' shock turned ta recognition. He took her lips in a tender kiss and caught th' soft cries as she rose ta meet him on th' mossy embankment, as he filled her with th' seed o' a god."

Alex moved closer to Brenawyn to look down into her expectant face, his voice almost a whisper, "Each full moon, he would meet her in his true form, gladdened ta see th' bairn quickening in her body. He showered her with jewels and treasure, insisting she'd keep them for th' bairn when she refused for herself. She never asked him for anything, knowing it wasna his ta give. In return, he didna ask about her life in the village, both knowing thaur was nothing ta be done. They'd make love softly, slowly, stretching it out ta remember each touch, each kiss, each embrace, ta hold them ta th' next full moon."

Alex paused, and it was Brenawyn who broke the trance, sighing, "How desperately romantic."

He shook his head to clear it and took a step back,

"Aye, I suppose."

"What happened when the baby was born?"

"Och tha's whaur it turns tragic."

"How so?"

"Ignorant minds o' men and th' rage of an Auld One. The bairn was ne'er born."

"Oh." Brenawyn frowned as she strolled to the East-facing standing stone. "How did the class respond?"

"Mixed reactions, but for th' most part like you."

She nodded and circled the stone, letting her fingers trace a prominent dark vein.

Brenawyn gave this thought as she strolled to the East-facing standing stone, "This is aligned with the rising sun?" She looked back over her shoulder and when he nodded, "Then it seems that this would be the obvious place to start, but I'm drawn to the North stone.

Walking to the stone, she placed her hand reverently upon it, "Yes, this seems right. Start with the North, then go…South...and then West…yes, yes, that's the way. Ending with spirit in the center"

She walked to the center of the circle and knelt. Brenawyn smiled and held out her hand. "Join me. You should know this better than I do. I don't know the actual words, if there are any that remain. But given your background, you would be the person to ask—but wait. This wouldn't be seen as disrespectful would it? I'm not a Druid, or even believe in any of this."

"No, it wouldna as long as yer intent was pure. Th' ceremony is one o' thanksgiving. All that is required is for th' person, ye, ta be thankful for th' bounty o' th' Earth."

"Well, I'm not a farmer. I didn't pick the fruit and vegetables I ate with dinner, nor did I slaughter the chicken. They were all bought from the supermarket, but I am thankful that it was there for me to purchase to feed my family. Do you think that counts?"

"Aye, that will dae, then. Society has come a long way since th' hunter-gatherer days."

"Ok, so are there any formal words for this?"

Surprised that she was so moved by his words that she thought she should try to abide by the ancient custom, he went to join her. Mimicking her posture, he reached for her hands, "Aaricht. Close yer eyes." She did so smiling. "And clear yer mind o' everything—all thoughts, worries, fears. Thaur is nothing but ye."

Pausing, Alex looked at her face and the slight lines in her forehead as they slowly relaxed. When her breathing changed to a deeper, more rhythmical cadence, he knew that she was ready.

"Noo, imagine th' grass; th' length, th' color, each individual blade." Opening her hands he placed them, palms down in the grass. "Th' grass is cool. And if ye were ta pick one blade it would give easily, but a clump or more is stronger. Can ye feel tha' strength? Even in each individual blade strength resides, springy and resilient; th' grass ye are sitting on, pressed doon by yer weight, will regain its form when ye leave. Noo imagine th' roots o' th' grass, matted and tangled just under th' surface. Vying for water th' sky gives, th' nutrients th' earth supplies. This is th' force from which ye must get permission." Taking her out of time and away from the modern conveniences, she could be a Druid preparing ta celebrate the summer solstice. "Noo, speak the words."

Brenawyn's brow wrinkled and she began to shake her head to which Alex interrupted, "Nay, thaur are nay words I can teach ye. They are from th' heart, Brenawyn."

Eyes closed she began, "Mother Earth, hear my plea. I come to you pure of heart and clear of mind to praise you. Grant me permission to give adoration in the Old Ways." Brenawyn paused for a moment and placed a kiss in each of her palms then pressed them into the grass.

The ground hummed with magic. There was no breeze, yet grass ruffled against her hands. The Earth rose to her call—*significant*.

He stared at her lovely countenance as a smile played at the corners of her generous lips. Did she sense it?

"Do you believe in magic?" she asked as she opened her eyes.

"I...um, aye. Magic is all around us, but 'tis subtle, usually," Alex responded, looking into Brenawyn's eyes again. "Are ye ready ta go back?"

Brenawyn shook herself, as if coming out of a trance, "Mmm, yes it's getting late." She rose, brushing the backside of her shorts as she did so. Brenawyn took a step towards him, but he backed up and refused to take her hand.

He needed to temper his excitement and quell his trembling hands before he touched her, so he shoved his hands in his pockets and said courteously, "I'll take ye home."

They walked back in silence, and Brenawyn was thankful for it. She was at a loss for words. Had she misread his signals? Did she do something that turned him off? He agreed to walk with her, then he had been telling her about the circle, and then…it must have been the circle. Did he think that she was being disrespectful? That wasn't her intention. Hesitantly she put a hand on his arm and stopped him, "Did I do something that angered you?"

Alex looked searchingly in her eyes, "Nay, o' course no'." He offered a half-smile and took her hand again.

As they approached the Rising Moon, voices raised in a heated argument pierced the stillness. "Doesn't that sound like Maggie?"

"Aye, it does. Shite."

"What's the matter?"

"I couldnae find the bastart streen nor the day…"

Brenwyn shook her head, "What?"

"Och," Alex pinched the bridge of his nose, and took a deep breath, purposely slowing down his rate of speech, "I apologize. I was looking for him. He laid his hands on her…"

Brenawyn stopped and grabbed his arm, swinging him around to face her, "He hit her?"

"Aye, innit wha' I've been saying?"

"God damn him! That son of a bitch! When I get my hands on him…"

"Thaur they are," Alex pointed to the shadowed alley opening a block and half away. "Listen, Brenawyn. When I get him awa' from her, take Maggie to yer place. Doonae wait for me. Once thaur, call the police."

Benawyn wasn't listening, and it was Alex's turn to grab hold of her arm to stop her from striding in half-cocked. "Brenawyn. Brenawyn. Repeat it."

"What?"

"Repeat it back ta me. Wha' are ye going ta dae?"

"Grab Maggie. Take her back to the house. Call the police."

"Guid. Let's go."

Brenawyn had to run to keep up with his gait. "What are you going to do, Alex?"

"I am going ta try to nay kill him."

They approached on silent feet. Buchanan had Maggie pinned against the brick wall, his hand a vise around her neck.

"Take yer hands aff o' her noo."

"Mind your own fucking business, old man," as Buchanan cocked his free arm back, fist bunched, ready to deliver another blow.

Things happened at once. Moving from next to her, Alex growled and tackled him to the ground. Without the support, Maggie started to sink to the ground, Brenawyn grabbed her, and pulled Maggie towards her. Maggie's small weight almost took them both down, but at the last instant Brenawyn's footing steadied, and with a quick backward glance, she saw the two men grappling for purchase on the ground, punches finding their targets. Brenawyn said a quick prayer for Alex, but did as she was told. She ran with Maggie, taking most of her weight the short distance to the Rising Moon. She fumbled to remove her keys from her pocket and get the door open.

Leo appeared at the top of the stairs as they entered the vestibule, and Brenawyn belted out instructions, "Call the police, get the med kit," as Maggie choked and wheezed, fighting to get air. "Jesus, we need an ambulance too!"

Topping the stairs, Brenawyn brought Maggie into the kitchen, where Leo had the med kit opened on the table. "Here sit at the table."

"No, floor. I need…" she gasped, "I feel—

"Okay, here let me help you." Brenawyn pivoted Maggie's body and got a hold under her arms, levering her to the floor with her back braced against the wall. Once down, Maggie started to wilt, Brenawyn caught her and cradled her head, "Maggie, sweetie, do you want to lie down on your side?"

A nod.

"All right, Nana, roll up that towel there and give it to me." She placed it under the girl's head. Maggie started to shiver. "Get me a blanket from the other room. Spencer, come here, boy. Lie down here." The dog sniffed Maggie and stretched out with a grunt, edging back so his body bolstered hers. Maggie was barely conscious, but managed to drape her arm over the dog.

The doorbell rang and Brenawyn and Leo stared at each other. "Did you lock the door, Bren?"

"I don't remember. Here stay here with her. I'll go and…"

"But what if it's him?"

"If it is, and I didn't manage to get the door locked? I need to find a weapon." She gained her feet and looked around the room eyeing the marble rolling pin on the counter. She reached the landing in three strides, brandishing the pin as a cudgel, but saw through the glass that it was Alex at the door. She flew down the stairs, ripped the locks open. She was surprised that she had not only managed to lock the door but throw the dead bolt too. She was in his arms as soon as the door was opened, feeling for injury, assessing his condition.

"Doonae dae that," he squirmed.

"Ooh, I'm sorry. Does that hurt? Do you think he's broken a rib?"

"No, ah'm no' injured, lass. It tickles is all."

Brenawyn pulled back to look him in the eye. "You're sure you're not hurt?"

"Brenawyn, ah am no' hurt. How's the lassie?"

"Oh, thank the Lord for small mercies. Maggie probably needs to go to the hospital. Nana's called 911. What of Buchanan?"

"Ah, the couart ran as soon as he could. It didna last long after ye left. I gave chase ta see if he'd circle back 'round. He's gone for the noo."

On the porch, after the police and the EMTs left, Brenawyn locked the door and turned to face Alex. "Do you know that your accent gets much stronger when you're upset?"

Smiling, "Aye, I ha' been told tha' it dae."

Brenawyn stood on her toes to plant a soft kiss on Alex's cheek. "Thank you, for what you've done for Maggie tonight."

Surprised by the sudden contact, he inhaled her scent of jasmine and roses, and before she could move away he wrapped his arm about her waist, pulled her nearer, and kissed her back. Her lips were soft and pliant and she melted into him. Taking this as a sign of acceptance, he moved to deepen the kiss, slanting his mouth over hers. She reached up to bury her hands in his hair, and he tightened his grip around her waist. Breaking off, he kissed her mouth, her cheek, her earlobe, and down her neck. Glancing up, he caught their reflection in the glass of the window. Her shirt had ridden up an inch or so and his hand partly covered the silky skin of her exposed back. On his hand and half way up his arm glowed iridescent runes. He stiffened and began to pull away. Brenawyn made a soft protest, but relinquished her hold on him.

Misreading the look on his face, she mumbled apologies, abashed by her wanton behavior. She didn't know what had come over her. Alex pulled her chin up so she was looking at him, "Doonae apologize. Let's go collect yer family."

CHAPTER 9

The morning of the ceremony dawned, and Brenawyn busied herself with her morning ablutions, deciding to dress in a white smocked eyelet sundress. She had returned to the room to put the finishing touches to her make-up when she went utterly still as she looked down on the dressing table. Guilt washed over her as she glimpsed a familiar gold ring settled in the velvet of her open jewelry box.

She slid on the ring, feeling its familiar weight at the base of her finger, and she was back there. Candlelight glowed in the cozy community church. *To have and to hold from this day forward, for better or worse, for richer, for poorer, in sickness and in health, to love and to cherish…* Liam brought her hand up to his lips as he slipped the ring on her finger and sealed it with a kiss. *From this day forward until death do you part.*

Death.

She ripped the ring off and shoved it in the bottom of the dresser drawer.

Her therapist's words echoed in her head. It was acceptable to begin to have feelings for another man. In fact, how many times had he urged her to start dating? Before, she felt that it would be disloyal, or worse yet, unfaithful to the man she claimed to have loved, if she were to date again. The fact that she hadn't had one thought of Liam this morning, or during the last week when she was with Alex, scared her more than the thought of dating faceless bland men whom she would quickly decide she had nothing in common.

Just a span of hours later, the memory of the vows she had made long ago again fell by the wayside when she walked into the office to retrieve the robe and took in Alex swathing his naked hips in a striking kilt of red and green plaid. Perhaps he didn't hear the click of the door over the din of the busy storefront? *What's the harm in looking,* she tried to justify in her head as she leaned against the door jamb, but a squeak from the damned hinges had Alex look up.

"Hello, Brenawyn." He finished belting the kilt and turned to meet her gaze. "Sorry, Leo told me ta use th' office ta change since I didna want ta walk from my apartment haur like this."

Her face must have given her away—it was on fire—because he sauntered over, lowering his voice to a flirtatious whisper, enjoying her apparent discomfort, "It causes too much trouble for my taste, with th' lasses swooning, and their men looking for a fight. Are ye in danger of swooning, lass?" he asked playfully.

Brenawyn rolled her eyes and gave a half-hearted attempt at an insouciant shrug, but she was too distracted by fantasies involving her tongue and the swirling tattoos in crimson and indigo that decorated the right side of his tightly-sculpted chest and abdomen. "Of course not. I don't swoon."

She tried to tear her eyes away, but they were drawn back to the red and blue, so vibrant, so very vibrant, on his golden skin.

"Did you just get these?" She put out a tentative hand, but stopped mid-reach as embarrassment hit. She was shocked that she had been about to touch his naked chest without an invitation to do so.

He closed the meager distance and trapped her hand against his chest. "I have had these for more years than I care to remember."

The pressure of his hand over hers relaxed and she traced part of a curve with a fingertip, "Do they have any meaning, or are they just designs?"

Alex stepped away, putting a hand to his rib cage. She could swear a look of sadness crossed his face, but he twisted to pace away into the small office. Reaching the opposite wall, he turned and leaned back on the credenza.

"Thaur's a myth about a man who was enslaved by Cernunnos." With a sweep of his hand indicating the tattoos, "These are the embodiment of the incantation to make him immortal, temporarily, to serve the god's will."

"What did the god want of him?"

"His continuing task is ta find th' god's daughter who was lost ta th' ages."

"Another child?"

"Ah, th' ways and will o' th' gods is no' for mortals ta judge."

"But why didn't the god go after her himself if he was so concerned?"

"Perhaps it was ta save her from fright. She didna ken

tha' she was th' daughter o' a god, and perhaps he was concerned tha' his countenance would frighten her."

"The daughter never knowing her father, the father forever mourning his daughter, and the man searching ceaselessly to find her, and he but a slave himself—very sad." Brenawyn considered the story. "The story is Celtic?"

"Yes, why?"

"Being an expert in the field of Celtic mythology, I thought you'd have a deeper insight into what it reveals about its people or their customs."

Carefully considering her question, Alex answered, "Perhaps it's a metaphor. Th' man ceaselessly devoted ta finding th' daughter o' th' god compared ta th' people's unerring devotion ta th' preservation o' their religion," shrugging his shoulder. "But in my experience, people tend ta complicate matters. Wha' would ye say if I told ye 'tis true?"

"Then it's even more tragic because it speaks to the futility of life. If it were true, I'm idealistic, and the romantic streak in me cries for the successful end to the man's search."

Alex bent to stuff his clothes in a rucksack and chuckled, "And I suppose ye want th' man ta fall in love with her, too."

"Happy endings are always good."

"Aye, they are, but rarely seen in th' tomes o' any mythology."

She scoffed, "Rarely seen in real life too."

"I am sorry about yer man." He rose to his feet, "Leo told me."

Oh God. I'm carrying on like a fool. I am married—was married, she corrected, *if only...* Tears threatened to flow.

Brenawyn glanced down at the desk when she heard metal strike the wood. Two gold armbands and a primitive scrimshaw neckpiece were on the desk. She reached out to touch it mainly to disrupt his attempt to pull her into his arms. *Don't touch me. Please, don't touch me. If you do, I'll start to cry, and shit, I might not ever stop,* she screamed in her head.

Alex stopped mid-reach, "I'm sorry ta ha' brought him up." He sighed, and reached to fasten the neckpiece on, but looked at it, considering, and handed it to her instead.

Accepting this distraction, she stroked the yellowed ivory and the cool gold caps, running her fingers along the engravings of a bear, a hawk, a leopard, and a wolf.

"Tis old. 'Tis supposed ta be th' ornaments," indicating the armbands as well with the swish of his hand, "o' th' last Druid Shaman."

Interested, she looked up, "Oh, Nana was telling me something about him," and blushed deeply when she remembered the context in which she'd heard of him.

Alex raised an eyebrow and a smile curved his lips, "I think I need to listen to yer grandmother's stories. They seem as if they would be more, hm, interesting than mine."

"So why would the shaman have it carved in this way?"

"According ta th' story, all shamans' torcs were made o' ivory ta allow for engravings ta be added as needed."

Brows knit together, Brenawyn started to ask another

question, but he continued. "It was said th' shamans could shape shift ta any animal they chose, but in order ta dae so they had ta focus on th' form o' th' animal, hence th' carvings. Th' shaman himself would carve th' likeness. To ha' another dae it would mean th' loss o' th' magic."

She was still admiring the piece in her hands when he reached for it, pulling lightly in the back. A clasp, cleverly hidden by the design, appeared.

"May I?" she asked, still determined to keep her thoughts occupied and keep Liam's ghost at bay.

He nodded and stood very still as she circled around him. Brenawyn brushed the ends of his hair away and placed the piece on his neck. She touched the clasp, hesitant to try to close it, lest she break the thing, but the slight touch snapped the torc into place.

He set the armbands—gold, silver, and copper bands woven together to form intricate knot work, snugly between his defined deltoid and bicep muscles.

She faced him again to look at the finished product. "Intricate tattoos and ornate primitive jewelry, an avenging god of an ancient religion—you're breathtaking."

"No' a god, but a warrior." He caressing her cheek. "But will ye offer me a boon?"

"A boon?"

"Hm, yes." He lifted a tendril of her hair. "A favor." And bent his head down toward hers.

Brenawyn's heart hammered in her chest. *Oh God, he's going to kiss me again. Please.* She put her hand on his chest, not sure if it was in invitation or warding.

He straightened and covered her hand with his.

"Aaricht, lass. Ye ha' some things ta sort. When ye're ready we will continue this conversation." Alex looked around the room, finding the robe hung on the back of the closet door, "Do ye need help?"

"No, give me a few minutes alone and then I'll be set," she said. She needed time to steady her heartbeat and slow her breathing.

"Watch th' time, though. Th' ritual needs ta be done at sunset or yer grandmother will have both our heads." Alex said while exiting the room.

Brenawyn heard a gasp and collective sigh following his exit. Silence reigned for a long moment and then titters and giggles were heard. Unkind thoughts ran through her head at the nasal voice that had the audacity to ask the clichéd question to a kilted Scotsman. Affecting a heavier highland brogue, Alex's requisite reply, "Och, lass, come haur and I'll show ye," had her closing the door harder than she intended.

She headed to the park in full ceremonial dress, obligated to accompany Nana to the circle while listening to her prattle on about the authenticity of the ritual being marred by the modern convenience of the wheelchair rented for the occasion. "Dr. Miller told you to stay off the foot. The two blocks to the park on cobblestone streets probably wouldn't do as much damage as the trek across the grass to the site. You could always stay here if you want."

Nana huffed and crossed her arms. "Lead on."

People thronged the street outside the shop, making the short pilgrimage to the park the next block over tedious. Inside, the robe was beautifully pagan, but on exiting the house and maneuvering the wheelchair down the porch steps, Brenawyn felt like a comic book conventioneer. But she hadn't looked up. When she did, her embarrassment was immediately allayed by the sheer variety of dress. A good number of people who were in route to the park were similarly dressed on a simpler scale. The rest greatly varied from over-the-top, stereotypical Goth attire which today included black candles and pentagrams, to the for-the-fun-of-it, exaggerated Halloween costumes, some of which looked to be expensive. The last group seemed to be comprised of regular folk on vacation armed with cameras to document their trip.

Alex was waiting as they walked up, and took Nana across the knoll, leaving her to casually scan the scene, checking to see if all was in readiness—stones, candles, and matches. She was happy to see that either Alex or Maggie had prepared the site. Colorful summer flowers sat in low vases and planters at the base of every other stone of the eight. The remaining stones had plinths decorated with the beeswax candles she had pulled from the stores' shelves. Fruits and grains adorned the ground surrounding the center dais as a sacrifice worthy of a ritual of thanksgiving.

By the time Brenawyn was finished assuring herself that they hadn't forgotten anything, people pressed in cheek to jowl trying to vie for the best vantage point. Looking at the enormity of the crowd, she was struck with the usual nerves that accompanied any public speaking engagement. Knowing from experience that she needed to start the show in order to find any peace from the nausea, she left her grandmother's side. With a pat from her grandmother for confidence, she began to walk the perimeter with a basket laden with the remaining needs for the ritual.

As Brenawyn passed first Maggie, then Alex, she took a deep breath, giving both a nervous smile. On the completion of one revolution she closed her eyes and began to weave through the standing stones counting her steps. Two more times around and she stopped, facing the East standing stone.

The moment she stepped within the circle, goose bumps raced up her arms and she shivered despite the warmth of the day. She approached the center offertory pedestal, turned, and knelt in front of it, giving a quick nod to Alex to begin his introduction.

Alex's baritone projected into the crowd, "Welcome. Join us in thanksgiving for th' Spirits' blessings. Lughnasadh is a summer harvest festival acknowledging and celebrating th' fullness o' life through th' bounty tha' th' Divine provides. Th' god Lugh created th' day ta honor his mother, Eithne. Over th' many centuries, celebrants ha' used it ta honor their mother, Mother Earth, for she is th' source o' all sustenance. 'Tis a time for purification and th' release o' pain, fear, sadness, ta allow a true renewal o' self ta bloom. Our priestess," turning to indicate Brenawyn, "is symbolic o' each o' us in adoration. She is committed ta her own purification and self-renewal, and by extension, ta ours.

"She will first call each spirit in turn ta acknowledge their power and favor in procuring th' harvest, placing a candle for each as a sign o' respect. Th' flame will remember our prayer, and th' crystal placed at th' base o' each will hold it bound. After, she will offer sacrifice—an offering o' th' Earth's bounty, and finally, she will pray for th' continued good will o' th' Spirits throughout th' next phase o' our year."

Stopping directly in front of her, Alex gave a wink and melted back into the crowd. Brenawyn took another moment to gather courage and stood, approaching the North-facing stone. Gathering up the hem of the dress, she knelt and ran a hand along the blue veined surface of the stone. It felt cool, smooth, and unyielding.

Courage.

Raising her arms above her head to the open sky above, her voice rang out in the gathering silence. "I acknowledge the North Spirit, who gives us true bearing, guiding and calling us home. I call to the wind, who lives companionably with the North giving us life-sustaining air to breathe." She reached for the amethyst. "I summon both to this circle. Let this crystal be forever etched with our plea." Placing it gently at the base she reached for the matches. "And the flame of the candle mark our prayer."

She tore a match from the book and struck it against the strip on the cardboard. It lit briefly, only to be guttered by a breeze, but before she had the chance to strike the match again, the crowd gasped. She glanced up, distracted, and glanced around at the scene beyond the stones. Wind beat against the spectators. Most were bent against the gale, sheltering small children, her grandmother and Alex stood in a similar position, Alex hunched protectively over her, blocking much of the wind. They squinted from the gusts as their clothes plastered themselves to their bodies. Both were staring directly at her.

The wind continued to batter them, but her robes were still. The wind whipped round and round, building momentum. There was a scream from somewhere in the crowd, babies crying here, people running for cover there. With a deep whoosh the wind changed; rushing from every direction and from all angles it entered the circle. The stones hummed as it passed their threshold and rocketed past her, the edges of her robe snapping against bare legs.

The wind converged on the offertory pedestal in front of her, and the wicks of the three white candles positioned there, blazed to life with five foot flames. Brenawyn whipped her head around, finding Alex as he bent down to whisper something in her grandmother's ear. She twisted to hear him and then both looked at her in unison with equal expressions of consternation and nodded stiffly.

She continued to look toward, not understanding what they wanted her to do. Finding no answer in their stern faces, she assessed. The wind was strange, but nothing, no one, was harmed. What could it hurt but to continue with this bit of theatre? "Come and reside with us, rejoicing in the coming harvest."

A force hit the flames from above, compressing them to pinpoints, painfully bright. A silent blast wave emanating from the three white flames rocked her back as it rolled over her. Brenawyn heard a whoosh and lifted her head in time to see all the candles around the circle were lit.

She stumbled to her feet, retreating from the North stone, the overturned basket forgotten. She took a couple of steps backward, but froze. That wasn't smart, heading toward ground zero. No. She moved in the opposite direction, intent on getting out. The demonstration was over, but as she neared, the candles' flames leapt, morphing the height of the stones. She cringed, fearing being burned. Brenawyn saw her grandmother standing now, clutching Alex's arm, both were mouthing something.

Why couldn't she hear them? She whipped her head around, straining. Why couldn't she hear anyone? It was only a couple of dozen feet. She ran closer. What were they saying?

Finish it? She shook her head not understanding. *Finish what?* Alex leaned over to hook Maggie's arm, dragging her toward him. Maggie looked startled, but agreed to whatever he had said to her and took his place, placing a hand under Nana's arm and freeing Alex to approach the circle.

Brenawyn stepped closer, flinching as she passed close to the candles, afraid of a possible flare up. She reached out as Alex approached, but there was something in the way. Smooth, cool—*glass?*

It can't be. It's impossible. Again and again, she tried, more forceful each time, until she was beating on an invisible wall, panic-stricken. Alex put out a hand and was met with the same obstacle. She saw awareness dawn on his face, and he motioned for her to stop. He bowed his head then braced his hands on the stones that stood an arm span's distance apart on either side of him.

He lifted his head and Brenawyn stumbled back in shock when iridescent eyes matching the emblazoned tattoos on his chest met hers. She could hear him, only him:

"Brenawyn, finish it. Finish th' incantation. Do it noo."

She took several steps backward and turned to run, casting glances over her shoulder at him. She gathered the basket and the strewn rocks and turned toward the South standing stone. She plopped the bloodstone at the base with no theatricality, then stole a quick look at her grandmother for affirmation. Nana sat in the wheelchair, her white knuckled hands gripping her knees. Alex knelt beside her with his right arm tense on the armrest of the chair. He looked ready to spring.

"I acknowledge the South Spirit, who awakens us to the promise and surprise of a new day. I call to the Earth, who provides a continual food source and the very ground we walk on. Let the flame stand as sentinel and this crystal be etched with our plea. I summon both to this circle. Come and reside with us, rejoicing in the coming harvest."

The flame of the South plinth burned green and the stone at the ground glowed. At once birds sang in chorus accompanied by the natural sounds from the various fauna in the surrounding park rising to an almost ear-piercing cacophony. Glancing around, members of the remaining crowd were holding their ears and small children cried. Hundreds of sparrows flew into the circle, bobbing and weaving throughout the pattern. The birds flew around the perimeter, following the same path of the wind, and at an unseen signal, the flock pumped their wings to gain altitude, clearing the top of the stones, flying higher above the circle. Still in sight, the flock undulated and soft downy feathers rained down as the birds molted in unison.

The featherless wings stopped flapping, sending bodies

plummeting toward the ground. It was so quick that if Brenawyn had blinked she might have missed it. The motionless wings multiplied with a tearing, two wings became four. Orange and black scales grew out of the plucked skin to overlap as they settled to cover the new wing structure. She squinted to get a better view...butterflies! Thousands of butterflies fluttered up on a breeze born in the South, mere inches before the first would have smashed against the earth.

They flitted about her, alighting in her hair, on her shoulders, chest, knees, and hands. She giggled as one brushed the side of her neck. In concert, those that had taken momentary refuge on her, lifted off at one time and congregated on the pedestal. They covered the platform and the candle entirely, posed there for a fraction of a second, and again took flight simultaneously, leaving a steady green flame burning behind.

A warmth radiated from her chest and fear was forgotten. Brenawyn regained her feet and strode to the West-facing stone. She knelt in front of it and placed the blue tourmaline at the base of the pedestal. "I acknowledge the West Spirit, who gives us comforting warmth and encourages us to seek new adventures. I call to the Water, who quenches our thirst and heals our wounds. Let the flame stand as sentinel and this crystal be etched with our plea. I summon both to this circle. Come and reside with us, rejoicing in the coming harvest."

Thunder boomed and lightning crackled across the sky as ominous storm clouds rolled in. As she finished the summons, the sky opened up in a maelstrom, pelting fat raindrops on the heads of the assembled audience, drenching them in seconds. Lightning struck trees on the perimeter of the park, sending limbs crashing to the ground, but now no one moved.

The candle's flame was still alive, if only a pinprick. But it flared likes sparks struck from flint when the punishing rain gave way to drizzle. Larger and more persistent it grew, despite the moisture in the air, spattering her and the entire circle in rainbows.

She lifted her hand, mesmerized by the prismatic colors of the kaleidoscopic candle on the plinth and the stone beyond. *Perhaps this is what the world looks like from inside a diamond,* she thought as her sleeve fell back to reveal the same effect across her skin.

Am I stone? Diamond? The same?

A heaviness crept into her limbs and the circle tilted drunkenly as Brenawyn gained her feet. Shifting patterns of color floated in front of her and swirled together in her wake. In front of the last stone, she fell to her knees, drawing out of the basket the obsidian and placing it reverently at the foot of the East-facing stone.

"I acknowledge the East Spirit, who gives us rest for our weary bodies to replenish our minds so we can again work the wonders of the Ways. I call to the Fire, who warms our hearth allowing us sight in the dark, and who is the full cycle of birth, destruction, and rebirth. Let the flame stand as sentinel, and this stone be etched with our plea. I summon both to this circle. Come and reside with us, rejoicing in the coming harvest."

From somewhere beyond the surrounding shimmer and

the perimeter of the stones, a flash of intense heat and light—different, harsh and more direct—burned away the dancing colors. She felt a matching heat at her back and turned to see a high flame spouting from the reflecting basin situated in the center of the circle. The flames jumped and caught in the high grass ringing the pedestal. Spreading outward in a concentric circle, the flames grew, consuming the green tender blades of grass.

Brenawyn turned her back to it, unconcerned.

In moments, tongues of fire lapped at the hem of her robes but she remained unmoved. She felt the heat, hot but not uncomfortable, but had no fear of being burned. She cupped a flame and held it in her hand, the skin of her palm untouched as the flame burned. The flames raced around her, burning their way to the edge of the stone, the entire circle engulfed now. She still sat within, waiting patiently for the flames to recede, her skin untouched, unblistered by the blaze.

A warm wind began to blow, and by the time she got to her feet, the flames died. The ground all around was scorched. A groan from the earth, and tiny blades of grass and weeds sprang forth, a phoenix rising from the ashes to replace all that was once green and fresh. When the dandelions bloomed, then set seed, the red flame of the candle for the East and Fire burned steady.

Brenawyn bent down to retrieve the near-empty basket and let herself be pulled towards the reflecting basin. Once there, she was compelled to place the last stone, the tiger's eye, in the center of the basin and began to circle the basin once, twice, and on the third time raised her arms once more and looked heavenward.

"I acknowledge the gods and goddesses of Old: Cernunnos, Epona, Belanus, Taranis, Blodevweld, Danu, and the Triple Mother Goddess. I offer my spirit to you. Let me be an extension of your will and of your Ways." The candles spouted high purple flames. "Let the flames stand as sentinel and this crystal be etched with my plea."

With what started out as a tickle of a feather drawn across the skin, soon turned into a tormented itching and by the time she pushed up her sleeves, her skin burned from within. Her hands and wrists were beet red. She blinked and saw something move under her skin. She gave a sharp shriek as purple marks appeared at her fingertips. The marks converged at the base of her fingers to coalesce into glowing swirls racing up her hands, wrists, and arms. Pulling the neck of the robe away from herself to look to see how far the damage went, she didn't actually see the flame turn colors, but knew they had by the renewed pain and the appearance of blue scrolls etched on her skin.

In turn, the flame turned red, green, white—and each time the color changed, new markings were added to her growing iridescence. Finally, the flames sputtered out and the pain subsided.

At the guttering of the candles' flame, she lost sight of the perimeter stones. She gave a brief thought to Alex, Maggie, her grandmother somewhere beyond. But now she was alone, standing in the warm radiance of the blessings of the Spirits and nothing else mattered.

"So mote it be." The flames of the candles marking the perimeter were extinguished simultaneously and she felt the energy leach from her limbs. Brenawyn's mind swam, registering physical exhaustion. She couldn't fight gravity's pull on her. She crumbled to the ground.

CHAPTER 10

Alexander felt the barrier of the veil drop, and he reached Brenawyn first, checked her vitals, and bundled her almost weightless body securely in his arms. Thoughts of calling for help never entered his mind. He didn't say a word or spare a look, but the crowd melted from his path.

Approaching the house, she stirred in his arms and wrapped her arms around his neck, snuggling deeper into his chest. He tightened his grip, holding her closer to him as he mounted the stairs two at a time. A shop clerk, whose name escaped him, was waiting, apparently apprised of the situation via cell phone, and rushed out to hold the door to the apartment for him. He didn't take the time to even nod his thanks, just headed upstairs. Her dog was waiting at the top of the stairs, nervous at his sudden appearance. Investigating the bedrooms, he discovered hers and closed her door abruptly on the inquisitive dog.

He bent to deposit her on the bed, but in her semi-conscious state, she nuzzled his chest and ran feather light kisses along his collarbone. He froze over her with a firm resolve not to take advantage of her in this state. He closed his eyes trying to get a grip on the situation, but the fact was she aroused him, and feeling her mouth on him felt too good.

She mumbled, "You smell like sunshine and grass." She grasped him closer as he reached mechanically behind his neck to unclasp her fingers. She cried, "Don't leave me."

He knelt at the side of the bed, placing her arms at her sides and reached to brush her hair away from her face, "Shh, I'm no' going anywhaur." He kissed her forehead and realized she was burning with fever—a fact that had escaped his notice with the exertion of carrying her back from the park. Rising, he smoothed her robe over her thighs for decency, and went to wet a towel in the bathroom.

Alex emerged to find Brenawyn gloriously naked, kneeling on the bed, crumpled robe and dress discarded on the floor. The glowing swirls of her markings accentuated her curves, sweeping out and around her body. His eyes followed the lines as they delicately decorated her breasts to their peaks, and interestingly merged again mid-abdomen to run down to the apex of her thighs, only to sweep out again with the flare of her hips. His mouth went dry and he dropped the wet towel on the floor, forgotten.

Brenawyn, eyes glowed with inner luminescence, her lips spread in a sensual self-satisfied smile as she noted his close perusal. In response she slowly stretched and raised her arms above her head and arched her back slightly to give him an unobstructed view. "You like to look at me."

He nodded in agreement, taking a step towards her. He burned to touch her, to cover her breasts with his hands, his mouth…to bury himself within her. It would be easy and a relief to give in, here, now…to surrender to the will of the goddess. Did it matter that she was imbued with the spirit of the goddess of fertility and not of a clear mind? Would she be as eager to mate with him if she was not? It mattered to him because somehow, he knew it would matter to her. It was this realization that stayed him.

He paced away, not very far in the small room, but turned his back toward her in hopes of getting a handle on his burgeoning desire. Bracing himself with hands on either side of the bathroom doorway, he tried to think of any number of random, sobering thoughts. He was so focused on this fruitless task that he barely registered the slight squeak on the mattress springs before he felt Brenawyn's supple body against his agonized one.

Alex pressed his forehead against the bathroom door jamb, trying to remember why it was a bad idea to enjoy her touch while fervently hoping she'd explore further. As if in answer to his silent plea, she reached down to gather the hem of his kilt in one hand as the other reached further and encircled his engorged cock.

She let out a throaty purr and began rhythmic pressure as she slid her hand up and down his shaft. He let out a groan and caught the reflection in the bathroom mirror through the open door. The reflection of what she was doing stilled him, and she peered around his shoulder to see what caused the change. She eased the pressure on his member, smiled luxuriously, and slid her leg up and around his thigh.

"Do you like this?" She tugged at his belt, and when it gave, the kilt fluttered away everywhere it wasn't caught between the press of their bodies. She lightly ran her index finger down the length of him; the act itself wasn't as shocking as the illumination of his sigils in response to her touch. The realization hit him like an electric charge.

"Interesting, isn't it?" She ran her hand elsewhere on his legs, abdomen, and chest; everywhere that she could easily reach, and the same reaction occurred—his runes glowed at her touch. "It's our individual wells of magic responding to each other." She stood on tiptoe and caught his earlobe with her teeth and whispered, "It's a sign that we are meant to be lovers."

Alex pulled away from her and turned, letting the kilt fall to the ground. Brenawyn smiled in response and towed him out to stand by the bed. "Alexander, I want you."

He took a step back, "No' this way, Aine."

Brenawyn cocked her head to the side, letting her hair fall over a shoulder, partially covering her right breast, and ran her left hand over her body, skimming the contours. She dipped her fingers, rubbing briefly between her legs, and quietly added, "I need you inside me."

Mouth agape, Alex backed up quickly, arguing with his baser instincts he reached down, scooped up his kilt, and belted it on. Only then did he face her again. "No, Aine, dae ye ken me a fool? This is wrong and I will no' be party to it."

Brenawyn-Aine straightened, "Ye will dae wha' has been foreseen. Ye and her," motioning to indicate the body she possessed. "Wha' we will, will be. Ye will dae as we command."

"I willnae dae this noo—this way. Ye may leuk like Brenawyn and sound like Brenawyn, but ye are no' her. She is no' giving her consent. If 'tis meant ta happen, that is, if we, *Brenawyn* and I, are destined ta become lovers, then I would ha' it that she came ta me on her own, not possessed by ye or any other divine being."

He bent to get the dress and tossed it on the bed. "Get dressed. I will be in the kitchen awaiting her kin. Doonae come out o' this room."

"Insolent cur. I will make ye suffer—"

"Impossible to make me suffer more," Alex murmured, but as he turned his back to walk out, Brenawyn-Aine scratched him. His reaction was too slow, and she swiped at his welling blood and touched his torc, activating his shape-shifting ability. "Damn ye, Aine."

"Ye will dae as we bid, beast."

The beat of his heart increased, thumping loudly in his ears, his chest, "Please, nay." Blood pumped to his extremities. "Tis no' enough ta ha' me? Must I…"

Dust motes hung in the air, the temperature of the room dropped infinitesimally: the onset of night, scents of lavender and rose hips from the potpourri on the corner nightstand, and of her, Brenawyn. Her scent. Her readiness. A ragged cry slipped from his throat. "I will no' defile her."

"Yer resistance is…interesting. How many times ha' ye been through th' resurrection, I wonder?"

"It matters no'. I am nothing more than a slave."

"Too much o' th' individual still remains. If t'were up ta me, I would strip ye o' it noo for yer insolence."

"Ye are bound by th' same laws tha' I am. More so, I'd imagine."

"Ye think me powerless?" Brenawyn-Aine pinned him against the bedroom door and ripped at her wrist, letting the blood fall on the wolf, bear, and leopard carvings of his torc. "For noo, let us see if ye can withstand th' three."

"NO!" but it was too late. Primordial instinct surged through him.

He grasped her about the waist and lifted. He saw her pulse quicken, her lips plump, her nipples pearl, he could feel the heat from her slickened core. It didn't take long. By the fifth thrust, he growled and spilled his seed into her.

Thought and reason seeped back as instinct dissipated. Brenawyn-Aine's self-satisfied smile filled him with self-loathing. Trembling, he gathered his kilt and left the room without a backward glance. He fumbled to the kitchen and vomited into the sink.

A few minutes later, Alex heard the front door open and Leo laboriously start to climb the stairs, her cast thumping on each step. She found him in the kitchen, arms still braced on the counter as he looked out the window. She approached, but he held up a hand. A chair slid across the linoleum and she sat with a huff. He sighed, turning to her to find her playing at the edging of one of the placemats, worrying it into a crumpled wrinkle. Wiping her eyes with a paper towel, she looked up expectantly at him, and then frowned when she didn't read what she had hoped in his face. She was silent for a long moment, searching his eyes.

"I will not lose her."

"Let's no' get ahead o' ourselves. Ye don't ken if t'will come ta that." Alex tried to soothe. "I ken ye ha' questions, but they ha' ta wait. The first thing we ha' ta dae is ta close th' ritual. All other issues must wait. The marks are still glowing. She is still possessed by th' Mother Goddess."

Eyes wide, she quickly looked down the hall to the

bedroom and then turned to Alex, her eyes narrowed, assessing him. She rose from the chair to cross the room and absentmindedly touching the knife block, asked, "Did you have sex with my grand-daughter?"

Whatever she had been expecting, it wasn't his silence. She turned to him, mouth agape, as she drew the butcher's knife. "How could you?"

He met her in three strides, and gripped her hand holding the knife, pressing it against his throat. "Cut me. Maim me. Kill me if ye think it will make ye feel better. It won't dae a bit o' good. I cannae die. I am th' Shaman."

"I know who you are, all the abilities you have as the man burdened with the mantle, but you are not immortal, Shaman."

"Aye, that is no' true, Leoncha. I am th' favored prey o' th' Wild Hunt. I exist for th' eternal entertainment o' th' gods. I ask ye ta put aside yer feelings for right noo because we ha' a more pressing matter. Tha' woman in thaur," gesticulating to the stairway, "is no' yer granddaughter. She may leuk like her, but her mind is no' her own."

Nodding her head as she processed this new information, Leo paced the floor. "But it's impossible for anyone but the caster to end the ritual. We'll have to wait until she wakes up and then walk her through it. Wait, do you know for sure that it's the goddess she's connected with?"

Alex nodded, "When I picked her up th' triskele[3] was traced in th' sand in th' reflecting basin and haur I've had

---

[3] A design of three interlocking spirals

some time ta study her markings. The interlace is broken by th' triskele and triquetra [4], both symbols for Aine, the Mother Goddess. As for ending it, 'tis possible. I can dae it. She isna prepared for this; her body is unaccustomed ta th' strain o' it. Why wasna she trained?" Alex stopped his question with a shake of his head and held up a hand, "Wait, doonae answer that, it can wait."

Leo stood in the middle of the kitchen, looking down the hall toward the bedroom, and then towards her stillroom, "I would need to reference my texts. I don't know how to end a casting not of my own making."

"Leo, I can end it myself—don't leuk at me tha' way. It wouldna end th' connection anyway, and afore long, I *will* be compelled ta return ta her. Brenawyn will be pregnant from my embrace afore tonight is done.

"Over my dead body."

"Ye cannae stop me—I cannae stop myself! Hate me, curse me—I deserve it. 'Tis nothing more than wha' I think o' myself. The longer she is possessed by Aine, the longer she is vulnerable. Aine kens my weakness. They all dae— and they'll use it, use me, ta meet their ends, ta satisfy the ancient prophecy. Leoncha, dae ye ken wha' happens after th' Hunt comes ta an end? Wha' happens ta th' prey?"

"Resurrection."

"Yes, but each time I come back different, with an additional ability which makes th' next Hunt more challenging. But each time, *each time* I am less a man. I am nothing but an animal who is more instinct than reason, a

---

[4] A design also known as the trinity knot

slave without a soul, without free will. A slave with captors who will see tha' a child results from th' union o' priestess and shaman because it ha' been decreed through prophecy. And Brenawyn will only remember th' encounter as a dream."

"She cannot have children." Leo said, almost as an aside.

This confession caused Alex to pause, but he quickly recovered, "Leo, tha' may ha' been, but doonnae tell me tha' ye think tha' being possessed by th' goddess o' fertility tha' she would remain incapable? No, she will get pregnant. Help me no' defile yer granddaughter further. Help me end this."

Leo looked at him, wiping away the beginnings of tears, and said, "Of course. Whatever you need, I'll do it." She put her hand on his forearm as he stood, and confided in a whisper, "She's the only family I have left. I'm an old woman, please don't take her from me."

Alex's face became hard, "Another time, but noo I need ye ta recreate th' placement o' th' stones. Ye are th' only one who can dae it because ye share a blud bond. Tha' bond will be acknowledged and honored by Aine, thereby allowing me ta transfer th' power that's coursing through her body."

"Maggie should be back with the stones and candles. I'll go and get them."

Alex was pacing the short hallway before the bedroom when Leo retuned with the box. He opened the door and she peeked her head around the jamb. Brenawyn was lying prone on the bed, the runes, in undulating luminescence, glowed in blending colors across her arms and shoulders. Leo looked down at her own outstretched arm, and her sigils flared to life. Her own pattern was not as intricate or colorful, but the placement was the same.

"What do you need first?" Leo said quietly as she put the box down by the dresser.

Alex approached and sat on the side of the bed, cradling Brenawyn's hand in his own. Electricity hummed up his arm at the touch, and she turned toward him and rotated her wrist so his fingers captured hers.

Her hand looked so delicate in his much larger one. His thumb traced the small callus on her index finger; her hand was otherwise smooth, with dainty fingers that ended in short, rounded nails. He could see the vulnerable blue vein as it passed from her palm to barely crest the surface of her wrist and then travel up her arm. She didn't look strong enough to withstand what would soon bring her world crashing around her. It didn't seem fair to tear her away from the life she had built, but he knew that she'd be lost if she stayed, if not dead, having no training and barely any knowledge of the Auld Ways.

Leo gasped at the marks glowing in tandem on their skin and looked up into his eyes for confirmation. "I should have known."

Nodding in acquiescence, he forced his attention to the patterns that decorated her arm. Once in lambent illumination, they grew, at his touch, to a bright radiance along with his own brilliant blue. He was so transfixed by the sight he did not realize Brenawyn was staring with equal fascination.

She startled him when she asked breathlessly, "Who are you?"

Catching her eye, he smiled and held up her arm, still linked with his, and caressed the skin of her forearm responding, "Interlace, we call it. There is a symbol for e'ery god in th' pantheon." He touched the nearest, "This triquetra is th' symbol o' th' Triple Mother Goddess." He caressed her with the back of his hand following the swirling path and came to rest on the next. "This path represents th' thread o' life eternal, th' crossings between th' spiritual world o' Tir-Na-Nog and our own. In yer recitation ye called upon Cernunnos, Epona, Belanus, Taranis, Blodevweld, and Danu. All are represented and linked in yer patterning."

"Who are you?"

"Ye ken who I am."

Leo gave him one scathing look in response, then set about recreating the placement of the stones and candles. Once the fourth stone was in place, the veil hummed with power. The dog hunched down and growled, hackles up in response to the stirrings of magic.

"Get tha' dog out o' th' room noo. He'll try ta protect her and harm her in th' process." No sooner were the words out of his mouth than Spencer lunged for him. Leo snagged his collar and dragged the belligerent dog out of the bedroom. She returned to squirm underneath the bed for the final placement of the stone. She grunted but moved as a much younger woman despite her injured foot as she stepped around to the opposite side of the bed to allow Alex to start.

Alex pierced Leo with a glance, and at once pulled up the hem of Brenawyn's dress to place his large hand on her abdomen while he slid the other in her bodice to cover her heart. Leo's eyes blazed with incredulity and outrage, but stopped when all of his scrolls ignited to brilliant life. They coursed down his clear chest and arms an iridescent blue; the tattoos on the other side glowed red with matching intensity. She was locked in his gaze and she saw the change from his clear blue eyes to iridescent. Fear replaced her initial thoughts of his licentious motives. Frightened by the sight, she reeled back from the power rolling off of him.

"Belanus. Belanus! Hear me." Alex shouted in his baritone. "Most revered Belanus, hear my plea. Intervene on behalf o" this child ta th' Mother Goddess and ask for both release and sustenance from her divine light."

The room grew warm, and a rasping sounded. On the heels of it, a breeze started to blow though no window was open. The breeze grew in intensity, forming a vortex which whipped around counterclockwise.

Knowing his initial prayer had been answered, he took a breath to address the Goddess herself. "Mother Goddess, please release yer child. In th' name of Belanus, who is most revered for enlightenment, I put myself, Alexander Morgan Sinclair, Druid Shaman, at yer mercy, dae with me as ye must, but release yer child, Brenawyn McAllister, from yer hold so she can bring honor to ye."

Brenawyn's body grew stiff as her back arched off the bed, then a huge exhalation escaped her lips as she slumped down again in relaxation. Her runes slowly melting towards Alex, whose hands held firm. The last of her luminosity dissipated as Alex's glowed painfully bright. Leo shielded her eyes. Breaking contact, Alex stumbled away, falling to his knees on the braided rug.

.

CHAPTER 11

Thoughts only for her granddaughter, Leo leapt at the bed, emotions in turmoil. She felt Brenawyn's forehead, cheeks and neck—no fever. Her breathing was slow and resembled the cadence of sleep. Leo patted Brenawyn's arm, relieved, and moved tentatively to Alex's kneeling form. His head was bowed and the glowing runes now shimmered, casting him in an eerie radiance.

Moving behind him, Leo touched his shoulder and he shuddered in response. "Doonae."

She moved to unclasp the torc at his neck, but his hand stopped her and tried to shove her away.

"Please, doonae. T'was all o' them. I cannae…I didna ken. Who…who is she? All o' them! Ye ha' ta get her oot o' haur. I doonae ken how much longer…longer I can hold on," he spit out in agony.

Leo reached into her shirt pocket to withdraw a pen knife and before he let her go, she twisted his arm and held it against his back and she cut him across the knuckles heartlessly. He hissed in pain and tried to pull the hand back, but she ruthlessly twisted and pulled it up further, letting his blood ooze over her hand. Quickly she transferred the sharp knife to her teeth and slashed the inside of her fingers. She spit the knife out and fumbled through his hair to the torc. She slid her torn fingers along the smooth inside of the piece. Then she grabbed his bleeding hand, untwisted the arm and ran it along the carved outside of the neck piece holding his hair out of the way. She released him, and Alex fell forward to catch himself on his hands.

She stood over him regarding the exposed torc; it and his neck were smeared with their blood. The carvings lit up one by one as their blood mingled. The precisely carved ivory details of the bear, hawk, leopard, and wolf stood out in contrast to the seeping blood as it collected in the grooves.

Alex was breathing heavily, his hair covering the array of emotions that splashed over his face: intense pain, rage, confusion, and relief. He could feel the power ebb from his body and calm settle over it. He slowly came to himself, and piecing together the details he deliberately sat up, and turned to find Leo with her hands on her hips looking like an avenging angel.

"Shaman, we will speak in the kitchen." She hobbled out the door.

Alex sat there, dumbfounded, for a few minutes, trying to clear his muddled brain. He stood on shaky legs, grabbed the doorframe for support, and gingerly walked to the kitchen, holding onto the wall to avoid falling. He found her in the room off her kitchen, two chairs already pulled up next to the counter facing each other. She sat when she saw him and handed him a cup of water when he approached. "Here drink this."

He did so obligingly.

"We have a lot to discuss and I'm not sure how much time we have until she wakes up. Before we begin, I want your word on several points. First, we only discuss this when Brenawyn is not around. Second, I say when she is ready to know everything."

Seeing his intended interruption brewing on his face, she leaned towards him before he even formulated the first word on his lips, "No! I am speaking now. I am laying down the ground rules." She looked over her shoulder at nothing. "Where was I? Yes."

Swinging back to pierce him with her gaze, "Third, Shaman, you will not force the information on her. She has not been brought up knowing the Auld Ways. She will wake up scared because she was kept ignorant—largely my own making, but nonetheless you will go slowly with her. Fourth, she gets to choose. If she does not want the responsibility, she does not take it on! And finally, fifth…" Leo's voice rose as she stood to lord over him, "You will not take her from me!"

"Agreed."

"Agreed? To all conditions?" she asked incredulously.

"I agree ta all o' th' conditions." Alex repeated. "Noo, sit doon and tell me wha' ye did ta me upstairs."

"From what I understood, you took the power of the incantation and transferred it to your own body." Stopping to collect herself she looked him in the eye. "I thank you for that. But you underestimated the strength and it was more than you could handle or," looking at him askance, "more than you anticipated given your short time of preparation. I know things like that take preparation. All I did was to release the power housed inside you to a more convenient location. I saw the torc this morning when you walked out of the office. I've heard of it, but I've never seen it, and of course, I thought it a fake until I saw your interlace."

"How did ye ken it would work?"

"For someone who is supposed to be omniscient, you certainly do not have a clue."

"No' omniscient, just a repository. Thaur is a difference."

Pursing her lips, Leo sat down. "The energy of the incantation, or the essence of the gods if you will, is directly linked to the earth and all things in it. The four symbols on your torc are the forms of the animals only, and because it is not linked to any one animal, the energy gets dispersed among all the animals of that form. Animals are closer to the gods because they lack the fundamental element that separates them from us—the will to choose. They can better handle this kind of power without it hindering them in any way. I'll demonstrate. Spencer, come here, boy." Leo called.

Tags jingling, the dog jumped off the couch and shambled in to sit by her feet, wagging his tail. "That's a good boy." The dog lay at Leo's feet. Pointing to the corner, "Let me have that piece of paper over there behind you." Alex reached over and handed her the sheet with a pencil he found underneath. Leo drew a crude picture of a dog, which looked surprisingly like Spencer despite its basic lines, and she placed it on the counter between them. Muttering words under her breath, she bent and repeated them in a whisper over the paper. The chant ended abruptly and the paper floated off the counter as a draft caught it. It landed near Spencer, and Alex could see his hackles go up. He lifted his head, sniffed the air and his tail began to wag slowly as if unsure. Another whiff of the air, the tail wagged in earnest, tongue lolling out of his mouth. He flipped on his back to rub on the carpet making doggie grunts of pleasure.

"The words of the chant aren't important here. The focus of the spell was Spencer and he had a pleasant reaction: the tail wag and the back rub. If you had been the focus, the reaction would not have been as pleasant because your free will stands in the way, resisting instinctual response. Humans have to meditate and prepare to quell the rise of their inner spirit. This was why you reacted the way you did. You did not suppress your spirit enough to allow for the essence of the pantheon."

Alex shook his head puzzled. "In all my experience, I ha' ne'er heard of tha' happening."

"Mmphm."

Alex rose and gave her a level stare. "Sit doon, Leo. I ha' some questions. First off, why don't ye seem at all surprised by today's events?"

Leo tried to hide behind the guise of tidying up. She was careful not to look in his eyes, but Alex gripped her shoulders lightly, trying to curb his mounting impatience, "Woman, sit doon and tell me wha' ye ken."

She sat, eyes locked on the piece of paper, intent on folding it repeatedly. "It has to do with the stones and Brenawyn's mother."

"Go on."

Leo began telling the story and soon found her

trepidation over revealing what had transpired that night relieved. "I thought something went wrong with the spell when she told me what happened. The stones exploded and were absorbed into the skin that protected the baby. I wasn't surprised that Brian refused me having any contact with them. The thoughts of what could have happened left me sick with horror. I deserved worse—much, much worse. So I didn't fight it. She was born later that night, healthy and robust despite being two months premature. I thanked the gods, goddesses, and whatever other divinity that watched over her. Knowing that she was alive and well…it was enough, even if I had to sacrifice being a part of her life to do it.

"Brenawyn's life has been filled with tragedy. Her mother died of cancer when she was nine, her father died of a massive heart attack when she was thirteen, then later her husband…I wanted to do what was right, to abide by her mother's wishes," she said pleadingly. "When Brenawyn came to me she was a sad little girl; it broke my heart. I kept her parents alive for her, raising her the way I think they would have wanted her raised. I kept my beliefs out of her upbringing and posed my store as nothing but hocus pocus designed for commercialism.

"I was taken off guard when I came down yesterday and saw the stones she chose for the ritual. She arranged them in the same configuration as I had that night twenty-nine years ago. I had never uttered a word about it, and her mother was too far gone with pain to notice. It sounds crazy, but can that knowledge be instinctual?" She looked into Alex's eyes searchingly.

"Perhaps. Nay direct record gives any insight ta explain wha' ye just described. We can turn ta th' prophecies, but then 'tis a question o' interpretation. They are so convoluted and vague tha' it makes it difficult ta pin down ta any specific person, event, or even time period. Let me think on it awhile though," he added.

"Come out back with me," looking over her shoulder, "I don't know how long Brenawyn will sleep and I do not want her overhearing our conversation."

~ ~ ~

Brenawyn awoke chilled and alone in her room. Unwilling to open her eyes and accept that she was conscious, she felt around for a blanket with her eyes still closed. Reluctantly, she opened her eyes to discover find she had been divested of the robe and lay on top of the comforter in her insufficient white, cotton sundress. She swung her feet to the floor and ambled over to the mirror. She stopped when she heard murmurings from the kitchen. Prioritizing, she opted for food over hygiene and turned to pad down the hall barefoot. The husky baritone of Alex's voice now intruded and she stopped to listen. She sat on the step smiling to herself; not yet willing to disturb the conversation as she listened to the cadence of his voice. She missed that…a male presence in her house. She couldn't hear what was being discussed, just the hushed tones of Alex and her grandmother.

Chairs sliding back on the linoleum and retreating footsteps indicated that Alex was leaving. She stood and proceeded into the now empty kitchen. Spencer was standing at the back door looking out. He wagged his tail when Brenawyn approached. "Hey, puppy. How's my good boy?" reaching down to give him a double pat on his side, "Stay!" as she wiggled around him to squeeze out the door. She pushed it open and closed it tightly behind her, then saw Alex and her grandmother still in conversation in the garden. She called out to them, but her voice was weak. She tried to clear her throat, but it was raspy and dry.

~ ~ ~

A white fluttering caught Alex's eye and he turned to see Brenawyn grasping the porch railing. He took the steps in a few bounds and led her to the wicker loveseat. "How dae ye feel?"

"I'm fine, just a little tired. I can't really remember what happened. It doesn't make a lot of sense, but I feel fine, like myself."

Leo mounted the steps to lean with her back on the porch post, arms folded tightly over her bosom.

"Hi, Nana. I'm sorry I ruined the ritual."

"Pussy Cat, you didn't ruin anything because it was just," waving her hand in the air noncommittally, "it was just fluff."

Brenawyn caught the frown that Alex flashed her grandmother, but she had no clue as to what it meant. "But, the crowd … and did I see right, was it being filmed?"

"Yes, but I'm sure they thought it was planned. Don't worry you did fine...just fine."

Leo returned his look with a self-satisfied one that clearly intimated something.

"What's going on?"

"Dae ye need anything, Brenawyn," Alex asked,

"afore I go?"

Her brows knit in confusion. "What happened?"

Not wanting to rush her by telling her things that her mind would rebel at, he probed, "How much dae ye remember?"

Brenawyn looked up and tried to recall, but only pieces of what seemed to be a fantastic and not-at-all-likely story came to mind. She captured his eyes again and the blurry recollection of a very naughty dream came to mind, she blushed and tried to look away. She closed her eyes. "It's all a blur and crazy images." Shaking her head to clear it, "I'm so tired."

"Sleep then." Alex brushed her cheek and assured her, "We will talk about wha' happened when yer ready." Leaning down, "I, for one, cannae wait."

"Why are you leaving?"

"Because ye need to rest. I'll stop in tomorrow to see ye. Perhaps then, if ye feel up to it, we can go ta sup." Alex offered.

"Yes, I would like that." Brenawyn responded.

"Well then, 'til tomorrow." He got up and placed a kiss on the top of her head. He turned to say his goodbye to Leo and she placed her hand on his arm as he turned to go.

"We still need to talk. You have a great deal to answer for," Leo whispered.

Meeting her eyes, "I leuk forward to it. Remember…read th' texts. The answers ye are looking for are thaur. Then we'll talk."

CHAPTER 12

Alex entered his apartment, quickly shoved the living room furniture against the walls, and rolled up the area rug to clear a space in the middle of the wood floor. Furious at the outcome of the events of the night, he couldn't focus even enough to keep his eyes closed, let alone regulate his breathing or slow his heartbeat for the necessary meditation.

The gods needed to answer for their actions. They were manipulative, self-serving, merciless. Frustrated and impatient, he lit five utility candles, foci he hadn't needed for five hundred years. He didn't even hold one shred of hope that he'd get answers. He was no one. A slave with no rights, no soul.

He placed the four candles at equidistant points and then carried the last back to sit in the center of the cleared space. There was a draft nearby and the flame of the candle in his hand, much like his concentration, fluttered, almost guttering, and then blazing, raging to life in hues of yellow and orange. He set the candle in the small holder a space away on the floor in front of him, but the candle tilted wildly. Taking it out, he dripped some of the melting wax into the cup, and then returned it, waiting a few seconds before letting go. The wax held and he sat back correcting his posture, and focused on the flame.

He stared at the flame, allowing the frustration and impatience to recede slowly. He breathed in measured increments, counting seconds before each exhalation and then again before he filled his lungs, all the while attentive to the consuming flame. He stayed this way for a time, but eventually felt the slow release of tension. He no longer had to count seconds before taking a breath. He turned to focus on his heart, imagining it thumping strongly in his chest, pumping blood throughout his body. With time, he felt the rate slow.

The strong draft died out and the flame leapt to life. The details of the room grew blurry and indistinct as Alex's living room, and his rented furniture strewn against the walls, dimmed. Mist appeared, slowly seeping in from the room's crevices, and tendrils reached out and encapsulated Alex; it roiled and swirled around his sitting form. The mist-covered living room floor gave way to a forest laden with lush vegetation, shimmering in pulsating waves, allowing glimpses that overlapped the diminishing view of the living room. This new scene coalesced in sensory detail as the other faded out.

Tentatively he breathed in the heady smell of crushed ferns, reached out to touch the tender fronds, heard the calling of birds and the rustle of brush as animals scurried through it, and finally opened his eyes to see glistening motes of dust float and settle around him. A soft pink light spread its dusky fingers through the dense canopy to kiss dew drops sparkling in rainbow luminescence on the surrounding foliage. He breathed deep of the scents of the forest and began chanting.

Grant me Thy Sight
Tha' I might see th' Truth.
In th' name o' th' Crone, who guides my wisdom.
In th' name o' th' Mother, who gave me birth.
In th' name o' th' Maiden who may come to love me.
I seek th' passion o' th' Lady.
I seek th' wisdom o' th' Lady.
I seek th' magic o' th' Lady.
I seek th' blessings o' th' Lady.
Grant me Thy Sight
Tha' I May see th' Truth
As th' Ageless Ones dae in Tir-Na-Nog
And all spirits both shade and light
On each day and night
Grant me Thy Sight
Tha' I may see th' Truth.

Cold prickled his skin as he watched the motes dance and swirl in the light, transforming into glistening, tiny, winged creatures. Wheeling and swooping in unison, they glided through the hazy light as if to a rhythm that only they could hear. Faster their wings beat, weaving in and out, as they flew closer to one another in tight formation. Light reflected off their mirrored wings projecting a kaleidoscopic image of colors and shapes before cleaving to form ethereal beauty. A statuesque woman with long, flowing, auburn hair that spilled over her shoulders stood before him, clad in a diaphanous gown glistening with a cascade of diamonds. Her face was flawless, with slightly slanted light blue eyes over high cheekbones, ending with captivating full lips.

Nimue, goddess of the Moon, waved an elegant hand and whispered to the wind, drawing Alex's attention to the vision of his other form sitting, legs crossed, back in his apartment living room. His mortal body fell to the floor in slumber, and the vision vanished, leaving him solely in Tir-Na-Nog. "Come. We ha' much ta discuss," she said as she turned.

Alex watched with fascination for a moment as she walked away, her dress fluttering in the breeze, her footfalls leaving no print on the forest floor. He fell into step a short distance behind her. Light punched through the canopy in places illuminating the flowers of the lush undergrowth against deep green shiny leaves. Birds sang in the trees even as the bear spirit emerged, an enormous grizzly with rippling muscles under its thick fur coat. Their eyes locked in acknowledgement and acceptance as the spirit fell into step with him.

A while later as silence continued to reign between the three, Alex heard the calling of the hawk, and looked up to see the spirit circling lazily in the sky above. The goddess and the bear stopped in tandem turning back to look at him. Alex braced himself as the bird dove and perched on his outstretched arm. It clacked its beak, ruffled its feathers, and tucked its head under its wing in relaxation. The bird sported the spectrum of browns and grays, feathers mottled and spotted on its wings, then fading to a warm ivory across its breast. Nimue gave a slight nod and strode ahead.

The woods they traveled through were changing now, becoming darker where overhanging branches reached to further intertwine, blocking much of the diffused light. Almost no light came directly from above; the floor was lit instead by bioluminescence emanating from the foliage. He could see his surroundings clearly still, but there were growing shadows. In the near distance, he heard a cat hiss and he knew that his leopard would be joining him in moments. The leopard appeared over the next hillock and waited from them to approach. The woman passed the animal, running a hand down its flank. Alex could see its soft spotted fur give to the weight of her hands and the surface muscles undulate in pleasure. The leopard's chest rumbled as it purred, falling in step with Alex.

Cresting a hill, he could see the last of his spirits, the wolf, waiting, eyes intently upon him at the edge of a clearing. The goddess entered the glade and called to the animal spirits. Only then did each leave his side to take positions loosely around her. "Do ye ken whaur ye are?"

Alex shook his head, "I am unfamiliar with this part o' th' forest."

"Of course ye are, child. Come with me." Taking his hand, she continued, "Just beyond this clearing, sheltered by hazel trees, lies th' Well o' Segais."

"Th' well o' knowledge. I thought th' it was just a myth."

"It has been sought more violently than th' Sacred Hallows: th' Spear o' Lugh, th' Cauldron o' Dagda, th' Stone o' Fel, and th' Sword o' Light together. In its depths, one can gain Knowledge. We ha' let it slip inta human myth after a millennia o' watching men kill each other over it. Th' quest ta find it, ta control it…" sighing, "We grew weary o' man's desire. It became predictable. The Well itself though…" She touched a low hanging branch lovingly and pushed aside the branches to reveal a lovely secluded spot, dappled in shadow. "The Well has always been haur guarded by th' forest."

Hazel trees ringed the small glen and sharp rocks were littered everywhere, but Alex could see that, at the center, water surged up from a narrow crevice in the Earth and bubbled over the rocks, collecting in a shallow pool.

She released his hand leaving him staring, mouth agape, at the famed spot. All of his recollections and the various myths he knew from all the sources did not prepare him for the complex simplicity of the scene. It was a peaceful spot, but he had seen others just as peaceful, maybe even more so. That was its strength. It was unremarkable to the practiced eye, and easily overlooked by the untried.

When he was finished gawking, he carefully picked his way through the maze of broken shards of stone and crystal to join her at the edge of the pool. "Ye had no need o' this knowledge until noo," she said as he squatted down next to her. "Ye were born with th' Shaman's abilities. It was yer ancestral right: All knowledge o' ancestry, practice, and ritual was reincarnated intact within yer memory. Ye, like all th' others afore ye, access it instinctually. Thaur is no memory o' when this ability came ta yer line, it just always has been. This has served ye in th' past; 'tis not enough noo."

"Tell me, was it desperation or fear tha' made ye act? That forced me ta… ta rape Brenawyn?"

132

"Rape? Ye didna force yerself. She initiated th' encounter."

"Aye, but would she ha' if not imbued with th' pantheon—

"It wasna all of us."

"Do ye ken tha' makes it better? Is it no' enough tha' I have sacrificed my life? Forsaken all earthly connection: wife, children?"

"Ye can still ha' tha'."

"Nay. Leuk at me." Alex implored. "I am eternal prey for th' Hunt. I am no longer a man. I ha' hunted and slaughtered on th' Grounds for survival; I ha' tortured and maimed others at th' behest o' th' pantheon. Feels like I ha' spent more time in th' form o' my spirits than as a man— felt th' rush o' soft vulnerable throats, felt th' gush o' blud when I ripped them open, th' bludlust... ah, th' bloodlust! My skin itches and my heart craves th' transformation, just thinking about it! Resurrected dozens o' times, I am stronger, faster; instinct rules, more than logic. I am no' worthy ta ha' a family. All it would take is for ye ta get th' notion ta turn me inta one o' these spirits in th' wrong place—I could kill my family, the one ye said I could ha' so nonchalantly."

Nimue reached down to draw her fingers through the water. Silt from the bottom stirred at the movement, swirling around lazily forming a transparent reflection of Brenawyn's bedroom. Alex's eyes grew wide and he leaned toward the surface of the water.

Brenawyn lay on the bed, her body curled slightly. Her dog nestled behind her legs, head resting on her thigh.

"Wha' ha' ye learned about her abilities?

"Nay, no' yet. Ye ha' identified her already as th' priestess. Ye used her as yer vessel and made me…tying her fate with mine and th' rest. Wha' if she is no' th' one?"

"Tell me, child. Wha' ha' ye learned?"

"She can call th' elements in a way only a few ever ha' been capable o'. Even though she hasna been indoctrinated, she is grounded and able ta quell her inner spirit, so she can be a vessel. Ye ken this though, but she kens o' our ways only as tricks and lies." Alex spouted as he paced away from her. "She has nay concept o' th' truth o' it and will likely violently refuse ta believe it. How will I convince her tha' she must go back?"

"Thaur is time. Observe her and teach her th' ways. She already has one o' th' priestess' five sacred foci in her possession, though it remains undiscovered. Ye must help her track down th' other four: the bracelet, ring, specter and athame. By the time ye find all, she will be ready."

"I am missing important information. Why would a normally innocuous ritual ha' such a strong effect on her? It should no' ha' been strong enough ta bring her latent abilities ta life."

"My son, thaur are many things ye doonae ken, things tha' were kept from ye."

Roused from his musings, Alex looked up. "Wha' things?

"This well has much magic, but it has been commonly misconstrued, and the most valuable asset of it has been overlooked." She held up a nut. "The fruit that sinks to the bottom is th' knowledge o' all things. To eat it," she cracked open the water-softened shell, "is ta open yerself ta that infinite knowledge. From the beginning o' time to its end, knowledge will always be power. In the Auld Ones' great intuition, they granted favor in this well, but it doesna come easily. For a prize such as this, th' effort of will is necessary to seek the truth."

She put the nut into her mouth and swallowed in two bites. A milky film began to creep across her eyes, and her voice boomed out ensorcelling Alex in a trance.

I ha' erstwhile seen woman taken and made with child,
By th' horned god o' th' hunt and th' wild,
Th' Woman blessed until th' day bled
And committed a deed most dread.

Sunk in mud in a ditch she cast th' Phoenix,
Worms and vermin th' only witness,
Cast from her th' child yet unborn,
To th' Winds of Change and Uncertainty torn.

In a rage, she was blighted ta serve th' rest o' days,
In Nothingness for her transgression and evil ways.
In a rage, casting exchange denied,
To th' Will o' Fate but not yet died.

I ha' erstwhile seen woman take and save her own.
With help from th' gods but to her unknown,
Five stones set a beacon ta a specific age.
And replaced a dying soul, so did th' mage

Th' destiny o' hope from tha' day,

Sleeping, waiting, innocent until wha' may.
So Chance intertwined th' fates o' those famed
To be rejoined and set right when legacy is reclaimed.

She drifted off, the eerie cadence of her voice disappearing, and it took a moment more for Alex to awaken from the trance. "Th' legacy reclaimed, that's obviously th' seat o' power; I ken this. Wha' am I no' seeing?"

"Time is fluid. All things happen in an instant. I can see when ye were born and when ye will die, just as I can see th' day o' the Earth's first dawn and its last. It is life, and for ye 'tis yer mortal coil—wha' makes ye and all of humanity so unique an' desirable."

"Aaricht, th' Phoenix cast th' soul o' th' woman's bairn out inta th' universe and it was called inta th' body o' another centuries later?"

"Th' Phoenix is a spell for willing sacrifices forfeiting their own soul for th' preservation o' our Ways. Upon completion o' th' soul transfer incantation on tha' fateful day, several banshee attendant ta th' nearby families heard th' desperate call for aid and, in chorus, began ta wail. Th' combined cry o' th' spirits was heard by all, including th' lord o' th' Underworld, who up ta this point kent nothing o' th' pitiable state o' his mortal lover.

"He didna comport himself well. He lashed out at his lover, Brighit, no' understanding her motive. Her captors fed by th' ire o' Cernunnos carried ta their ears by th' winds o' change, they starved, tortured, eviscerated, and then burned her alive. They were increasingly incensed by her hold on life, living in ignorance of th' forces tha' manipulated them and kept her alive. It was…brutal.

"After th' rage o' th' Horned One settled and he found reason once again, he found tha' she had done it out o' love—perverted th' ways intended for th' working ta offer her child a chance. It was too late for her. Ravaged by mortals and her god, she sits in th' Underworld endlessly screaming, recognizing no one. It is said tha' he goes ta visit her daily, holding her as she screams, hoping tha' one day it will stop, and she'll recognize him, and be able ta find peace. In part, th' quest ye are on has roots thaur. He thinks that if she sees th' girl, she will recognize th' soul and find peace in th' fact that her ultimate sacrifice of body, mind, and spirit was no' in vain.

"All things happen in th' same instant, as I said afore. Th' other spell was worked in ignorance, but th' same desperation rang out through time. So as Brighit was casting th' Phoenix, and th' banshee were singing their dirge, th' other gods saw th' true sacrifice of both women and bade it be so. Th' innocent soul cast out found a home in another in need. Th' reason th' ceremony o' thanksgiving had such a profound affect was tha' fate recognized th' soul through th' precise stones used.

"This emotion, love, has th' capacity ta break down th' strongest and strengthen th' weak—most curious. These emotions…they seem ta be more compatible with mortals. Th' sheer force o' love intertwined these two bludlines. It has combined and strengthened th' link.

"Both children were fated ta take their place within th' Auld Ways. Each was gifted with her own separate affinities and talents. Those two lines are entwined within one body and spirit through th' actions o' others, because o' love. This female, whom ye ken familiarly as Brenawyn, is th' strongest high priestess o' Druidism in th' record o' time, but her abilities are unknown ta Fate. Her legacy must be reclaimed. All is dependent on it."

The wind shifted and the animal spirits raised their heads to it. The surrounding forest became still. Motes of dust and leaves falling from the trees hung suspended, birds were pinned motionless in the air, the Well of Seagais lay tranquil. The animal spirits gathered tight around Alex and stood at the ready—hackles up and teeth bared, facing outward. At once they bellowed, belting out a plaintive lament that shook the ground.

Nimue stood, and for a moment she was shrouded in tiny sparkling motes that were once the gown; now with a toss of her head, the gown was replaced by resplendent jeweled armor. "Go. The Vate is close. They will find her."

Alex fell back on his living room floor, gasping for breath, drenched in sweat. He was unprepared to be forcefully hurled through the veil between the worlds; his chest constricted and he lay prone on the floor until the stabbing pain subsided.

"Did ye ha' a nice visit with yer mother?" Cormac yawned.

With a hand still clutched to his chest, "Cormac! Do ye no' hold with locked doors? Maybe as a message that yer no' wanted?" Alex gained his feet and advanced upon his unsolicited visitor.

Cormac sat back in the chair and shooed Alex away with a wave of his wrist as he casually assessed the apartment's door over his shoulder, "Well, that's o' nay concern and if ye truly wanted to keep me out, ye would ha' used a stronger barrier and layered the wards." A smile played at his lips as he shifted positions to sit on the edge of the seat, "Tell me, are ye getting old? Ability slipping perhaps? I always disagreed with th' decision ta pass th' mantle o' Shaman ta ye."

Alex had once counted him a friend, but that was long before he was chosen. They had grown up together in the same village, competed for the same pretty lasses, though Cormac tended to go for those that Alex's good sense told him to steer clear of. There was none that could take them if they stood together in a fight. If that was all there was, it should have been all that was needed; Alex would have thought himself lucky to have the love of a good woman and the bonds of brotherhood. But then came the vows. Pompous arrogance, or rather ignorance, spoils a righteous cause. Alex and Cormac were both narcissistic and blindly turned the staid initiation ceremony into a parade when they had heard that it was to be overseen by the goddesses Aerten and Caer Ibormeith.

They had taken the vows kneeling shoulder to shoulder in Tir-Na-Nog, and were branded as part of the warrior's caste securing them places amongst the Coven to uphold the traditions and practices until the priestess was found. All would have ended well if not for Cormac's daft-headed idea to call out Caer to have her relay the prophecy; and to add to it, Alex's senseless notion to reach out to stop her when she didn't pay Cormac any mind. He knew his mistake immediately and the thought of it now still made him tremble, as she rounded on him, her light blue eyes already clouding over with the vision.

I ha' erstwhile seen ye Shaman made,
By yer ill-advised actions many years will fade.
Hunted and hounded, separated from wha' ye hold
most dear,
Joined in th' eternal Hunt ye shall find fear.

Set free only at th' Hunter's caprices,
Compelled ta seek th' lost one.
Hunting throughout every nation,
Will wha' ye find be yer destruction or salvation?

Alex remembered every word, for they had sealed his fate.

Aerten herself presided over the Rite of the Phoenix in the next hour. Prophecy and Fate together, one to foretell and the other to make it so; no wonder people tended to steer clear. The previous Shaman only held the office for twenty-three years. Gray hair hadn't even begun to grow on his head.

He remembered Cormac's face at the proclamation and ceremony. It didn't change. The envy was almost palpable—almost as great as the hatred Alex read in Cormac's smug countenance now. Cormac couldn't bring himself to move beyond it then, and their friendship had dwindled soon after. He saw it as the gods' favor, not as the death sentence it was.

"I've no' had the time ta dedicate ta replacing th' spells ye so callously shattered. I did make contact with th' woman, though o' th' one who intervened I've learned nothing."

"Nay. It doesna matter noo. It appears tha' th' gods ha' found her."

"Ye were in th' crowd yestereve."

"I saw ye carry her back. Verra interesting tha' incantation was, aye?"

Alex rubbed his temples, trying to get a hold on his annoyance. "Wha' dae ye want?"

Cormac snickered, "It looks like ye weren't needed after all. When dae ye think ye'll be called back to the Stalking Grounds, noo that ye ha' proven yerself incapable o' e'en identifying a mere potential?"

Alex balled his fists, but Cormac was up and took a wild swing. Alex easily ducked and came back with a solid left blow to his jaw, followed by a right to his ribs. Cormac staggered back and lost his balance against the coffee table. He splintered the pressed wood table as he fell.

"Do ye want more, Cormac? Ye ne'er could best me at hand to hand. Wha' makes ye think ye can dae so noo?"

"Truce." Cormac held out his arm. "Help me up."

Alex clasped his forearm and yanked.

"We must make arrangements ta present her ta th' Elders."

"Book yer flight and go home, Cormac. Take th' Vate with ye. She's nay longer needed."

"Wha' o' th' woman?"

"I will take care o' her. I will stop by to pay my respect ta th' Oracle afore ye go."

CHAPTER 13

Roaches skittered across the tiled bathroom floor, so Cormac couldn't even say the motel was clean, despite the overpowering smell of bleach in the confines of the motel room. He closed the door and looked over at the snoring form of the Vate, unconscious since the moment her duty was done. She lay curled on top of the bedclothes in the same position since she was deposited there. At least the dead eye was closed.

He paced, wearing the orange shag rug further, occasionally stirring the thick green concoction which she insisted having after every read. She finally began to stir. He strode over, helping her to a sitting position as he handed her the elixir. "Haur, drink this, it will soothe th' pain."

She slurped greedily at the foul smelling potion, licking her top lip to get the last of it.

He sat on the side of the bed, spreading an afghan around her skeletal frame, "Tell me, wha' did ye see?"

"Our path is unclear." Shaking her head, "Multiple visions, all dependent on th' actions o' others—Sinclair, her and ye.

"Could ye see if she's th' one? Or are we wasting our time yet again?

"Only tha' she's someone o' import. Too many variables. Ye must put aside yer difference with Alexander. We must keep him close, manipulate th' information he receives, use him, and then if necessary, ye can kill him."

"Ah, if it were only that easy. I kill him, he'll just come back stronger and more arrogant."

"The apprentice's botched attempt, acting, I think, on yer behalf. Aye, he cannae be killed, he is forever part o' th' hunting grounds. So it is noo, at least, but in time? Until then, observe th' courtesies and respect yer betters."

It rankled to hear Alexander considered his better, but she was right, Cormac had to bide his time until the moment he could make Alexander pay. "Wha' shall I dae when he comes ta me?"

"Ascertain wha' he has learned and then encourage him ta stay close, learn wha' we ha' been unable ta see. Encourage him ta train her."

"And about th' other matter?"

She rounded her eye on him. "Th' acolyte needs ta retreat. He cannae be found by her—not yet. It is still unknown wha' his portion is in th' prophecy, but when it is made clear, 'tis easy enough ta call him forth. Send him back in time, Master Bard. He deserves a reward, if only for a moment, for his devotion ta our cause. He served us well by diverting attention from th' sacrifices."

~ ~ ~

Alex had to meet with Cormac again and quickly, before they retreated to Scotland and disappeared into the murk. At daybreak, he ventured forth.

He closed and padlocked the door to the apartment's

143

attic and opened the attic window sash. He undressed, folding his clothes neatly to pile them on the edge of the wardrobe. What would he tell Cormac? The instinctual response urged him to flight as his bones hollowed and plumage settled around his body. He might not even get to utter one word.

The foreknowledge of Cormac's limited funds led him to the sole motel in the area. He perched on the apex of the main building, where a blinking neon sign advertised vacancy. A screech from his lungs sent a curtain twitching at the end of the long U of cottages. The door opened, Cormac looked his way and hurried off with a bundle under his arm.

Alex found the pile of clothes: sweatpants and a t-shirt, under a tree behind the motel. The door latch gave when he knocked, sending the door swinging in, squeaking on its hinges. The Vate hunched on the end of the bed. Cormac, arms crossed, leaned against the closet door.

"Alexander," he nodded in his direction. "Ha' ye new information?"

"I have. She's no' th' one we search for."

"The gods seem ta disagree. Do ye doubt their power?"

The Oracle turned her milky eye toward him, smacking her lips together several times before speaking, "Shaman, th' omens ha' been vague and contradictory. While we cannae afford ta be hasty, th' fact tha' th' gods ha' recognized her gives credence ta our efforts."

Cormac handed him a vial of silver nitrate, "Come Shaman, show us wha' ye ha' discovered." Leading him to a plastic ice bucket filled with tap water, Alex worked the cork free and emptied the contents in the bucket, swirling it with his fingers. The water became cloudy instantly, and then a vision appeared. Recognizing Brenawyn, Alex wanted to hide it, throw the basin on the floor, eliminate her face from where Cormac could see.

"Ah, a verra pretty wench. Perhaps, I will take yer duties off yer hands."

"Nay. Nay, it falls ta me; my obligation."

"Oh, but ye are weary, rest this one out, I'll take care o' her. Eliminate her from th' list o' potentials."

"No, Cormac. I will dae it."

Alex didn't hear the Vate approach from behind and cringed when she touched his arm, "Have her in Scotland and ready by Saimhain for her presentation ta th' Elders. It must be done ta complete th' initiation rite so she can take her place, long absented."

Peeling off the borrowed clothes, "Until October then."

CHAPTER 14

At 7:45, dressed in a black sheath dress that ended just above her knees, Brenawyn tossed her heels by the back door and opted for the more comfortable flip flops. No need to begin torturing her feet by putting the strappy heels on before Alex arrived. "Nan, I'm taking the kitchen garbage out, and I'll bring the cans to the curb for tomorrow's pick up." She went to put a new liner in the kitchen can.

"Ok, Brenawyn. Thank you. Will the dog be okay while you're gone?" Leo asked from the living room.

"I'm taking him out with me now. He'll be fine until I get back." Brenawyn said in response. "Come on, Spence. No time for a walk tonight. You'll have to make do with the back yard."

Spencer bolted out the screen door and Brenawyn went around to the side, reaching over to unlatch the gate. Stepping out, she stuffed the last bag into the plastic bin and dragged it to the curb. She stood looking down the street with her arms folded over her chest. Goose bumps prickled on her skin as the branches of the nearby trees rustled in the cool wind. A man in a hooded sweatshirt hurriedly walked past, eyes focused on the ground. She stepped out of his path quickly to avoid collision. She stared after him but he never looked up. Shrugging her shoulders, she bent to get the community paper on the front steps and heard Spencer growl.

Paper in hand, she rounded the corner of the house and saw the dog clawing at the fence to get out, "Hush, Spencer. What's the matter with you? I'm..." A hand clasped roughly over her mouth and the other latched onto her waist like a vise, lifting her off the ground. Her scream was muffled by the restraint, and she clawed at the hands, writhing in his grip. She bit down on the fingers that found their way into her mouth. The assailant tore his hand away bleeding, and ripped at the neckline of her dress. The flimsy silk gave way at the shoulder seams, and panic flooded Brenawyn's senses. Mouth freed, she took a deep breath and screamed. The assailant renewed his efforts, grappling as he forced her through the gate, away from prying eyes.

She hit her head on the slate walk as he pushed her to the ground. Momentarily dazed, he had time to straddle her hips, grinding them into the ground. Sprawled on top of her, he captured both her hands in one of his, and held them pinned above her head as he groped in the pocket of his sweatshirt with the other. His hood came free and to Brenawyn's horror, his eyes flashed scarlet under bushy brows and heavy lids.

With a deep snarl, a blur hit him mid-chest, knocking him off Brenawyn. She scrabbled away, scooting back on the cement using her legs as propulsion and only gaining her feet when she reached the wall of the house. A long-bladed knife glinted with the reflected rays of the near-setting sun as the attacker faced eighty-five pounds of teeth. Spencer launched himself in another attempt at the man, but the knife sunk in the vulnerable side of the dog. Spencer fell to the ground in a whimper, blood spurting out to coat the brindle fur.

"NO!" Tears streaming down her face, armed with a rock pried from the edge of the garden, she flew at her attacker, but he was too quick and dodged. The rock only grazed his shoulder and he emitted a grunt; but in the next instant, he seized her again. "NO! Please, my dog," she cried.

He brought the knife to her throat and pressed until she could feel a slow warmth trickle down her neck. She stilled, praying for her grandmother to stay safely inside, for someone else to hear her struggles and call for help, for Alex to come and scare him off, for her dog not to die, for a quick death, all at once. Straining her eyes, she looked at Spencer's labored breathing, but with a shudder his chest ceased to heave. She closed her eyes as fury and bile rose in her throat and she bore down with white knuckles on her attacker's bare forearm, the sweatshirt pushed up in their previous struggle.

~ ~ ~

Scents of burning hair and roasting meat reached Alex's nose before an ear-piercing shrill scream broke the silence. He rounded the corner at a dead run and ran into a man clutching his arm. He struggled with the man, wrenching the arm away from his chest; the fleeing man howled in pain, all fight leeched out of him. Alex looked down; the man's skin and the flesh underneath his fingers had been burnt away and charred to the bone. Alex released his grip but the damaged flesh tore free, and a renewed scream erupted from the hoarse throat. Alex backed away to watch the man stumble off.

Hearing a sob from further back in the yard, Alex ran to find Brenawyn crouched over her dog. Her sigils glowed brightly down the long line of her near naked back, but it was only on closer perusal that he noticed that her exposed skin was covered in bleeding scrapes and red welts that promised to be bruises tomorrow. "Holy sh—did tha' man…? I'll kill him." Alex shook with outrage.

"No, help me. My dog…my puppy. Help me. He's hurt bad."

He dropped to his knees beside her as she pressed what appeared to be the remnants of her dress, wadded up, to the flank of the bleeding dog. Tears flowed freely from her eyes in dark rivulets as they tracked her make-up down her cheeks. "Help me, please. Spencer was stabbed," she sobbed.

He ripped off his jacket and placed it gently around Brenawyn's naked shoulders, then he reached to rub the dog's head. Spencer weakly wagged his tail. "Tha's a guid sign. Afore we try moving him ta th' house, did ye see him stabbed?"

"Yes, but not very clearly. The knife went in just behind the left shoulder, but I couldn't tell how far it went in, or the angle. The blood was spurting out. That's bad, isn't it?"

He lied, assuring her that it wasn't, and assessed her condition. The runes glowed in a pulsing radiance up her arms, across her chest and abdomen and her hands emitted a bright blue light as it pressed the cloth to the dog's side.

"Did he hurt ye…more?"

"No." Looking down at her bruised body, "he didn't hurt me more than you can see. I don't know what he would have done if he had no distractions though. He was too strong."

"Thank th' gods for small mercies tha' yer dog was a distraction. Let's try ta take th' dress away ta see, because we're going ta ha' ta ease th' pressure ta move him."

Brenawyn took her weight off the make-shift bandage, and the dog gave a small grunt of relief. She eased the cloth back to reveal the gash, but the bleeding had slowed considerably, welling to fill in the gap, but no longer gushing out.

"Aaricht, I will lift him. Grab his muzzle gently but firmly, I doonae want him ta bite me as I move him."

She positioned herself by Spencer's head, the dog's eyes rounding on her dolefully. She cupped his chin and gently placed her thumb over his muzzle.

"Rise with me." They stood in unison, the dog securely braced in his arms, its soft cry the only sound between them. "Och, tha's guid. Ye can let go o' his muzzle. Go clear th' way."

Brenawyn picked up the wicker basket on the step. She was only a step of two ahead of Alex so she opened the kitchen door and ran to clear the kitchen table with a swipe of her arm, letting the pot of silk flowers bounce and roll away. "Put him here and I'll get the first aid kit."

Leo entered the room as Brenawyn ran out. "What is— oh my goodness!" she cried striding to the table side. "Alex, what happened?"

"Go get a clean towel," he barked over his shoulder.

As Brenawyn hurried back with a pile of towels and compresses, Leo took in her granddaughter's appearance—dressed only in her bra and black slip, bedraggled by blood, mud streaked over her limbs and back, her dress obviously the bloody rag held to Spencer. She watched as Brenawyn impatiently discarded Alex's sport coat over the nearby chair to rifle through the medical kit unhindered. "This is useless. I can't use anything in here," she said throwing the kit on the floor.

"Haur Leo, gi' me a clean towel," Alex calmly said over Brenawyn's shoulder. Then, taking Brenawyn's hand and pulling her closer to the dog, he directed, "Haur, put pressure on it." Once she was positioned, he stepped away, taking the blood soaked garment from the table and dropping it in the sink. He ripped at his tie, unfastened the top two buttons of his white shirt, and rolled his sleeves up past his elbows.

Slipping the tie beneath the dog, Alex tied a temporary field dressing to keep pressure on the wound. Stepping back, he noticed that the cadence of Brenawyn's speech changed from the soft murmurs of tender endearments to her wounded dog to higher pitched, almost hysterical mumblings, causing Alex and Leo to look at each other. "What's the same, Brenawyn?"

Brenawyn looked over her shoulder, "The eyes. His eyes were the same—the same as the woman at the rest stop."

"How were the eyes the same? What woman at the rest

151

stop?" Leo and Alex asked simultaneously.

"I thought it a trick, play of the light, an overactive imagination when her eyes glowed red."

"Whoa, start at the beginning." Alex turned to face her. *So she's rationalized the encounter with the Vate. How much will she remember now? Will she recognize him? Perhaps it would be better if she did.*

Brenawyn took a breath, "I stopped at a rest stop on the way here to use the bathroom. It was empty when I entered, but not for long. The stall next to mine was occupied by a person who shuffled in. The person, the woman—you have to understand, I have no proof that it was her—grabbed my ankle underneath the wall. I stepped on her hand I think, to get away and ran back to my car. Spencer was barking and snarling in the car, and as I drove away, the woman— because I swear there was no one else in the bathroom at the time—she stood in the roadway watching me pass. Her eyes glowed red. The dog went insane, jumping to the backseat, foaming at the mouth much like he did tonight."

"Did you call the police?" Leo asked.

Brenawyn looked at her grandmother flatly, "And tell them what? That some woman grabbed me in the bathroom, and later her eyes glowed red?" Brenawyn quipped sarcastically. "No. I didn't call the police. Once Spencer calmed down and my heart stopped racing, I dismissed it."

"Tonight, your attacker's eyes glowed the same red?"

"Yes. Don't look at me that way!" Brenawyn looked to her grandmother and said in a small voice, "Nana, I am standing in a room and everyone's eyes—do my eyes glow too? I'm assuming here, since my skin does. What is that anyway?" She looked at her outstretched arms. She saw the identical nods, "All right, everyone's eyes, including my own, for some unfathomable reason, glow...if not for that, I would have thought I was crazy too."

"Go wash up and put some clean clothes on. I'll take care of Spencer. We have to call the police."

"No, first I have to take Spencer to the vet to get treated and stitched, then I'll call the police." Brenawyn said flatly, leaving the room. With a tired sigh she stuck her head back in. "Alex, can you take care of Spencer for my grandmother while she looks up the address for a vet?"

"Aye, lass," he said, taking Leo's position.

When Brenawyn returned, her grandmother was just hanging up the phone. "It's in Danvers, not far. I have directions. They are expecting you."

Brenawyn reached over to kiss her on the cheek. "Thank you. I'll have my cell if you need me. Lock the doors and set the alarm. I don't know when I'll be back."

CHAPTER 15

Brenawyn left the vet's office, reeling in astonishment that the knife had only caused minimal damage to Spencer, and that the vet had said the blood vessels had constricted to stop the bleeding in a way he had never seen before. The vet wanted to keep him overnight for observation. The police were called because a stabbing had to be reported, and by the time Brenawyn and Alex pulled up to the house they had mapped out what to say. The two police officers leaning against their vehicle and speaking in hushed tones were obviously waiting for Brenawyn.

Brenawyn left Alex at the car and approached the policemen, ready to tell them as much as possible: There had been an attacker. He had stabbed her dog and assaulted her. No mention of red eyes and glowing limbs. No mention by Alex of the attacker's arm being burned to the bone. She took the officers down the side yard where Spencer had jumped into the fight. She gave the physical description of her attacker, sans the glowing eyes. He had been short, a few inches shorter than she, dressed in blue jeans and a hooded, oversized sweatshirt; a tattoo had decorated the right inside wrist, which she'd seen when the sleeve was pushed up, had been tattooed with three thick ink lines, the outer two at opposite angles to the center.

"The tattoo detail will help narrow it down. Did you recognize him?"

Retracing their steps, "No, I didn't recognize him." She quickly added, "I'm new to the area. I've visited in the past, but I've only been in the area for a couple of weeks this time. I have stayed close to home and... I'm sorry; I know it's not much help." Tears rolled down her face. Alex approached and put his arm around her.

"Sir, when did you arrive during the attack?"

"I was walking ta th' house, I bide just up th' street at 67 Church, ta take Brenawyn ta dinner. I heard a scream and ran, only ta run inta th' feckin' man fleeing th' scene. Had I kent..." he said, disgusted with himself. "Och, no matter. It was then I heard Brenawyn cry out; I went ta th' back and found her and th' dog."

Officer Henderson stepped closer and commented almost accusatorily, "It's funny, sir, that no one else heard anything, don't you think?" He pointedly scanned the street, "This street is typically not crowded at that time of day, but people are around—at the restaurant there, and going in and out of the coffee shop, not to mention the bakery across the street. No one heard anything. The buildings are close together, and noises, such as screams, often seem louder at night."

Spine tensing, Alex said warily, "Officer, am I under suspicion for this crime?"

Breaking away from Alex's hold, Brenawyn took a step forward, "No, it wasn't him. I have told you that the man was considerably shorter than me," she interjected coming to Alex's defense.

"No, sir, it appears that the lady is comfortable with you." Then turning to Brenawyn, "It's all right, ma'am, if you remember anything else, be sure to let us know. You need to come down to the station to sign the report tomorrow afternoon.

Brenawyn and Alex walked into the kitchen to meet Leo, who was wringing her hands and pacing the linoleum floor. Brenawyn gave her a weak smile, and turned to kiss Alex chastely on the lips. "Thank you for your help tonight. I'm sorry that our date was ruined."

"Doonae thank me." Alex reached down to brush a stray curl behind her ear, "If I'd got thaur sooner he wouldnae ha' hurt ye."

"Shh, don't blame yourself." Brenawyn looked down and reality sunk in. The sweatshirt hid most of the abrasions, but she pulled it from her skin in revulsion. "I have to shower. Can you wait?"

"If ye would like me ta, I will."

"Please…Nana, can you help me upstairs? I don't think I can get the sweatshirt over my head without hurting."

"Certainly, Brenawyn. Head upstairs and I'll be right there." She waited until she heard the stairs creak before turning to Alex. "Can the two incidents be related?"

"Leo, I was thaur at th' rest stop."

"What? How did you happen to be there? At that time?"

"I was tracking th' Vate. I kent her ta be in th' area from reports o' occult occurrences—they make headlines. I ha' been tracking her for months noo, ever since I found tha' she's taken a hand in finding promising candidates."

"You don't know that Brenawyn is—"

"Do ye ken how many women over th' centuries? Dozens, and they all need ta be considered." He paced away. "Something's happened tha' has changed th' rules. I doonae ken wha', but th' procedures for divination are not being adhered ta any longer."

"What did you do exactly at the rest stop?"

"Not nearly as much as I was prepared ta dae. It wasn't warranted. I dropped th' veil, assured tha' it would ha' th' desired effect when I saw th' dog. I wasna disappointed. Tha' would ha' been it, other than following her, forcing an introduction, and then eliminating her as a contender based on her aptitude, but th' Vate arrived afore I did and I had ta go see."

"She doesn't remember you though?"

"Nay. Even though she ran inta me, she wouldnae because she was afeart. Then after th' rest stop, it was more important ta follow Brenawyn, but I lost her on th' road and figured I'd ha' ta triangulate her position. Dump th' truck and track her. It was just chance tha' she was coming haur."

"When were you going to tell me?"

"Leo, yer taking things oot o' context. Wha' dae ye think I am? I wouldnae ha' said anything until I was sure. Noo tha' we ken she is th' Vate's next target, she must be told. She is no' frail or feeble o' mind. She kens and has accepted more than ye give her credit for. She will adjust."

"Be that as it may, she's still my granddaughter," Leo said resolutely, then sighed, "It will be a long night, Here, catch," she said as she tossed him the keys to the shop downstairs.

Leo looked at him, her lips a grim line bright against a too pale cheek. "The towels and washrags are in the hall closet, then go down and get a shirt off the shelves. After you're done, bring your shirt and we'll burn it with her dress.

CHAPTER 16

Leo quietly entered the bathroom to find Brenawyn slumped on the wide lip of the tub with her head against the painted wall. The sweatshirt was in tatters on the floor, the scissors still bearing the traces of clipped fleece lying on the edge of the sink. She looked up through eyes too wide and dark set in a face that was slightly sunken. Her cheekbones pressed against her pale skin and dark shadows had developed under her eyes.

"I'm sorry." She gave a small smile and sat up, "I got in here and took one look at my reflection and I couldn't stand the thought of ever wearing these clothes again. I needed them off me immediately." She bent to clean the mess, but Leo knelt and bundled the sweatshirt up carefully to cover any blood stains and pulled it away.

"Hush, it's all right. I've got it." Leo responded, clutching the bundle to her abdomen so her shaking wouldn't be as obvious. "I should have come up sooner."

Brenawyn absently waved away her concern, "No, it was better that I was alone." She looked away. "God, I need to scrub my skin until I feel clean."

"Do you need any help?"

"At first I thought I did, but now, having it off me, I don't feel so nauseous."

"All right, I'll get you some towels and the lavender soap. Do you want me to pull out your nightgown and robe?"

"Yes, please, then we need to talk. Is Alexander still here?

Leo nodded, "Yes. He's cleaning up." She turned as she was leaving, "Brenawyn, please call if you need help dressing."

Leo heard the faint sound of the shower as she descended the stairs to talk to Alex. The back door was open and she found him sitting quietly on the wicker loveseat on the back porch. She moved to join him, and he scooted over to allow her to sit beside him. "Is she aaricht?" he asked.

"She's in shock, I think,"

"Understandable. 'Tis one thing ta ken tha' violence exists, but 'tis quite another thing having ta experience tha' violence personally. It's a shock th' first time. With repeated violent experiences, th' shock dulls."

"You seem to know of what you speak," Leo responded quietly, eyes drawn to his face.

Alex nodded, "It distances ye from th' act." He paused for a long moment then sadly continued, "It was better for me ta ha' it so, considering my task. I wouldnae wish it on Brenawyn, though."

"Why would you say that? I would think that having some mental distance to violence would allow you to think clearly, without letting fear cloud your thoughts."

"On the surface yer correct, but thaur are repercussions ta it too. Suffice it ta say, I am no' connected ta life anymore. It doesna matter ta me if someone is cruel or violent towards me. Pain fades. But throughout th' years, it doesna matter if they are gentle and loving, either. Life happens around me, people grow, they get old, and they die—but not me. I am a fraud. I ha' interacted with people, women. A'm sairy. They are fleeting, and I ha' ne'er allowed myself ta get too close. People ha' family, friends, relationships—but not me. Wha' could I offer ta any o' those? I cannae ha' a lasting relationship with anyone because my sole purpose for living for 660 years is ta find Cernunnos' daughter, the high priestess of th' Auld Ways."

Leo reached over to grasp his hand but said nothing. They sat that way in companionable silence for a while then she turned to him, "What are you going to do now?"

"Leo, I ha' ta show ye something. Do ye ha' a flashlight?"

"Yes, it's in the kitchen, I'll get it for you." She moved to retrieve it but Alex's hand on her arm stopped her.

"Whaur is it?"

"It's in the first drawer under the counter next to the dishwasher." Leo said resuming her seat on the wicker loveseat.

He returned after a moment with the flashlight in hand, "The shower is still running but we may no' ha' much time. Come with me, it's in th' yard." Alex stood and helped Leo descend the porch steps, careful not to rush her. Once to the bottom he let go of her elbow and walked to the spot where Brenawyn was attacked and flipped on the light, handing it to Leo when she approached.

"Shine th' light haur." Alex squatted in front of the

161

light and looked up at Leo, "This is whaur her blud was first spilt on th' ground."

"Wh...what is that?" Leo asked, bending forward to get a better view while keeping the light focused on the same spot.

"Ye want me ta take it slow ta be sure about Brenawyn, but Leo... we doonae ha' time." Picking up a double handful of the substance on the ground, he stood, bringing several dozen dead earthworms into Leo's sight.

Gasping, she took a step away, "But, you can't... there are many ways to interpret an omen. How do you.... how can you know if it's the correct interpretation?"

Dropping the worms on the ground, "Come. Ye ha' ta see something else." Alex walked to where the dog had collapsed. "Shine the light haur."

Leo hesitantly did as she was told. Illuminated in the light of the flashlight were foot-tall grass and flowers blooming in profusion. Speechless, she scanned the surrounding newly-cut, well-manicured lawn and realization started to dawn. "Is this where Spencer fell? Where she tried to stop his bleeding?"

"Ye ken th' answer ta that. She saved her dog's life haur. The residual magic she used spread oot underneath and around him, prompting th' growth o' th' grass and th' flowers. She needs ta be taught noo, afore something else happens. Tonight's events should be reason enough."

Leo turned her back to him and walked a distance away. She looked up for a long moment at the lighted bathroom window. Alex could see Brenawyn's muted silhouette against the frosted glass of the window.

Leo turned, "Come back into the kitchen." Without aid, she climbed the stairs, slamming the screen door as she entered.

When he reached the door, she had already seated herself at the kitchen table. She looked up at him when he entered and gave a tired smile. He sat across from her.

"Earlier, you asked why Brenawyn was raised the way she was. Love was the reason. Brian Farraday, the man my daughter married, was a religious man, a devout Fundamentalist Christian. He accepted the way Margaret was, but he was never going to abide his daughter being raised that way. After Brenawyn was born he changed. He threatened us, that if he ever found out that we were teaching her the ways, he would make sure that we would never see her again. He had the money and the connections to do that. He found out my role with the protection spell. He took them away for years—eight long years, the longest of my life. I would get packets of pictures every so often, just stuck in an envelope, no letter attached or return address. Then one day they were at my door, the three of them. I never asked her what made him change his mind because I was so happy that I could see my girls. Brenawyn didn't know me. She was reserved and shy. She took a liking to my cats and carried them around, one under each arm, and at night they lay curled around her sleeping form."

Alex smiled. "So she always had an affinity for animals?"

"Yes. Oh yes, it seemed like they followed her home. Cats, dogs, birds, rabbits, once a silver fox, you name it. I have seen her sit in the garden with dozens of butterflies flitting about her, or other times when sparrows landed in her hand."

"She still thinks she's ordinary after tha'?"

"Of course, I can do that too, and so could her mother. On a smaller scale perhaps, but that was all the evidence that she needed." Leo looked up. "Don't look at me that way. I was afraid that he would take them from me again. Just because he changed his mind about letting me into her life didn't mean that I wasn't afraid of Brian's doing it again, and this time permanently. So I enjoyed them until Margaret became ill. I tried to help, talk her into going to the doctor at least, but she didn't want any of it. Brian was eerily reticent about it. He would leave for longer periods of time, and during one of these absences, she died in her sleep."

Alex put his hand on her arm, rubbing gently. "Parents shouldnae outlive their children."

Leo nodded her head and pulled her hand away. "There is a reason I am telling you this." Alex nodded. "Brian was contacted and he came back immediately and then after the funeral, he took her away. He went into her bedroom where he found her with the cats. I was standing behind him. He tried to pry her fingers from the cats' fur, the boys took exception to this rough treatment and hissed and clawed him, causing Brenwayn to nestle deeper in the blankets and their fur. I told him to let her take the cats. His first response was a curt "no" over his shoulder. The tears from her eyes softened him though, and he released his grip, sat back on the bed and asked her if she wanted to take them. She sniffed and said that the cats had names, Frick and Frak, and they wanted to go with her. She let them go, brushed back her hair, and ran her hands over her face wiping away the tears. She came over to me, slipped her hand into mine and pulled me over to the rocking chair. I sat down, and she climbed into my lap. Brian sighed and went out to the kitchen leaving us to sit like that for a while."

"Then you sat me up." Leo and Alex turned at once, surprised to find Brenawyn in the doorway, "wiped my face with your handkerchief, kissed my cheeks, and said that you would miss me. You stood me on my feet, went over to the bed and handed me Frick and Frak. Dad took me from you that day, and I didn't return until four years later—to stay."

Brenawyn stuck out her bare foot, wiggled her toes, and laughed. "I'm sorry; I guess you didn't hear me come down. I always could sneak down those stairs."

"Come sit with us. Can I get you anything?" Leo asked pushing back the chair to stand.

"Don't get up Nana, I'm fine." Brenawyn answered, taking a seat at the table. "And I feel much better now. I'm glad you're still here, Alex. I have a feeling you are involved in this, but I don't know how, yet. There have been strange things that have happened since, and neither of you seem all that shocked. Maybe I'm paranoid and in need of therapy, but you two seem have had secret suspicions confirmed. Don't look at me that way. I've seen the looks that you two have shared. Now is the time for truth. What is it?"

Leo's eyes fell to the table and she heaved a sigh and muttered, "I don't even know where to start…. I never wanted this to happen."

"Like it or no', it's happened. Tell her wha' she wants ta ken; wha' she should ha' kent all along," Alex admonished.

Leo turned blazing eyes on Alex, but their fire was soon banked by a look of innocent confusion from Brenawyn. "Honey, I don't want to bombard you with information without giving you time to acclimate. Let's start with answering your questions. You have questions, don't you?"

Brenawyn turned to Alex, sat back in the chair and folded her arms over her chest. "Okay, who are you? And I want the real answer. I'm not buying the whole visiting college professor gig anymore, because something isn't quite right here."

"I am wha' I ha' claimed. Check with th' personnel department at th' college if ye need verification. As for th' rest, ye ha' an idea. Ye saw evidence o' it a week ago. Ye just refuse ta believe yer memory—convinced yerself tha' yer eyes played tricks on ye again. Th' woman at th' rest stop and yer attacker tonight were linked. Aye, Brenawyn, th' glowing eyes were real. Just as it was real when ye saw th' glowing runes on me; they were glowing in response ta ye. It wasna a figment o' yer imagination. Ye doonae need therapy."

Alex stood and stepped away from the table, "So ta answer yer question, I am something more than a college professor. I am th' protector and keeper of th' lore of Druidism."

Whatever Brenawyn had expected it wasn't this. She looked at him and then at her grandmother and burst out laughing. She laughed so long and hard that her sides started to ache. "Oh God, thank you, I needed a laugh after tonight."

She stifled a recurrent case of the giggles when she recognized the identical masks of reprimand worn by her grandmother and Alex. "What? Oh, come on, give it up. Things like that don't happen. Nana, your eyes have appeared to glow in the past, but you already have exceptionally bright blue eyes. Truth be told, it's a really good trick, I could never fathom how you did it, but I suppose the right amount of tears welling would make them seem brighter."

"What did I tell you, Alex? She is skeptical."

Pivoting around in the chair, Brenawyn looked at her grandmother with her mouth agape. "Do not tell me that you believe him, Nana? I mean come on! This is not one of your stories—this is reality, for Christ's sake!"

Leo threw her hands in the air and firmly commanded, "Show her," and walked out of the room. Alex stared after her for a moment, lost in thought, and then brought his eyes to bear on Brenawyn, who still sat in the chair, eyebrows raised, staring at him incredulously.

He opened his mouth but Brenawyn interjected before he could utter a word, "Wait, before you say anything…it's too much, too complicated. I am putting a stop to this. I thought I would go out with you tonight and have a good time…probably have a wonderful evening. You are a very attractive man and God knows how long it's been since I've been on a date, but now I see that it wouldn't be that simple. God, it's never simple! If I'm not delusional then you are—

either case is a recipe for disaster. I'm sorry." She stood and slowly moved backward towards the hallway door holding herself tightly with crossed arms shaking her head. "I would like you to leave now."

"If ye decide ye doonae wish ta pursue it then I will accept yer decision. But, please, allow me ta show ye—ta explain wha' is happening ta ye. Afterward I'll leave if ye wish it."

Leo returned to the kitchen to find Brenawyn in the doorway, "Listen to him. I know you're frightened, but he's not going to hurt you."

"How…how do you know?"

"Shhh, hush now. Everything will be all right." Leo's eyes lighted on Alex, "Here's your bag that you left the other day in the office." She threw it to him and it landed at his feet. Alex bent down and grabbed the bag, tossing it further out of the way.

"Don't be frightened now. I'm here." Leo soothed, standing beside Brenawyn with a strong arm around her waist.

"Nana, I'm so confused. There are so many questions and blurry memories from last week that don't make sense. I can't voice them for fear I would convince even myself that I should be hospitalized, or at the very least heavily medicated."

Leo nodded in commiseration, "Alexander has the answers to all the questions you have. But it appears that you are not yet ready to listen to them. That's ultimately my fault. The way you were raised…the way that I continued to raise you after everything that happened with your parents. I thought I was doing right by you, but it turns out that I did a grave disservice instead. Once you finally know everything, I'll ask you to forgive me."

"There's nothing to forgive, and even if there was something, of course you would have my forgiveness. I love you." She fiercely hugged her grandmother.

Breaking away and stifling the tears streaming from her eyes, Leo asked, "Alex, do you need anything?"

"Nothing," Alex replied as he dropped to his knees in the middle of the clear linoleum floor. "Brenawyn, try ta remain calm."

Eyes locked on Brenawyn, Alex mechanically stretched the t-shirt over his head. She tried to turn to her grandmother for explanation, but Leo silently reprimanded her and indicated that she should watch. Uncomfortable with the idea, Brenawyn tried to shy away, looking down at the floor, at the kitchen table and chairs, anything rather than to look at his naked chest. But the instant he started chanting her eyes sprang to his face.

The torc that she had seen at the summer solstice lay around his neck and the steak knife that had been on the table appeared in his hand as he sliced his fingertips on his right hand. She hissed in response to the pain it must have caused, but he didn't react to it. He threw the knife on the floor, and it skidded to a stop under the table. Chanting louder, he ran his bloodied fingertips along a section of the torc.

The air in the room sizzled with electricity and the chanting stopped suddenly as muscles moved under his skin. Brenawyn, fascinated by the sight, moved to step closer, only to be stopped by her grandmother. "Don't. He needs room."

Sitting back on his heels, Alex threw his head toward the ceiling, as the muscles continued to shift. Bones began to crack and elongate and he threw himself on hands and knees, arching his back. His hair fell to cover his face, so Brenawyn couldn't see the agony registered there. Dark hair sprouted from his spine and spread covering his naked back and his tattoos. The fabric of his pants ripped and rags fell to the floor as the form of man shifted to wolf.

The wolf shook himself as if shaking off water, and the last of the transformation took shape. Long fur hung from its tail, haunches, and neck and when it finally raised its head Brenawyn stared into familiar iridescent green eyes. The hair on Brenawyn's arms stood up as she gasped for air and tried to reel backwards, taking Leo with her into the hallway and imagined safety. Leo hung on and forced her back in the chair, seemingly unperturbed by the appearance of the wolf.

Leo took her chin and forced her to look at the wolf. "Brenawyn…Brenawyn, look at him. Look at Alexander Sinclair, Druid Shaman, shape-shifter. This is only part of what he can do." Forcing her chin back, "Brenawyn…Brenawyn, do not fight me. This is not the time to be hysterical. You must accept this."

Leo released Brenawyn when she ceased to struggle, and looked at the wolf, "I suppose she won't believe until she sees you turn back. Here, I'll get your clothes out." The wolf looked at her with his head cocked to one side and one ear positioned toward her, the other flopped on its side. It sat and let Leo edge around it watching her as she retrieved the bag and laid jeans over the back of the chair." Then looking back, "Are you sure that you'll be all right?"

Brenawyn started to answer but was cut short by a sharp bark from the wolf. Looking over her shoulder, "I'm sorry Brenawyn, I was speaking to Alex." Turning back to the wolf, "I think she'll be okay now. She doesn't look like she'll run, anymore." Turning to leave the room, "Brenawyn stay there. No one here will hurt you."

Slow creaking steps could be heard as Leo ascended the stairs. Brenawyn's turned her attention back to the wolf, who sat non-threateningly on his hip, leg stretched out to the side, mouth spread wide in what appeared to resemble a doggie grin. After a moment, the wolf stood to move closer, but Brenawyn cringed away. The wolf sat back down. For endless minutes, it went on this way, the wolf ambling closer, then sitting at any indication that she would run. Finally within Brenawyn's reach, the wolf sat again, whined, and edged closer. She looked at him and tentatively stretched her hand to his head. The wolf closed the distance and she pulled back squinting her eyes shut. The wolf lifted his paw and put it into her lap, waiting patiently. Once sure that no violence would befall her, she opened her eyes and reached out to pet his head. He whined happily and tried to lick her hand. The shock of contact with a tangible impossibility had her eyes roll back in her head as she slumped to the floor.

When she came to, it was to Spencer nosing in her hair. She cautiously opened her eyes only to be confronted with her hallucination again: not Spencer but the wolf.

171

The wolf stepped back and shimmered. Before Brenawyn's eyes the transformation back to man, back to Alex, was made. He crouched on the linoleum. He stood in his naked glory and smiled into Brenawyn's horrified face.

"Leo, Leoncha, she's going to bolt. Leo, get in haur."

Shaking, heart pounding, Brenawyn got to her feet and turned to rabbit to the only other exit, through the store, but her grandmother appeared blocking her way. Brenawyn grabbed her and yanked, but Leo was stronger than she looked and held her ground.

"Brenawyn, Brenwyn, honey, Stop. No one is going to hurt you."

"Nana. We have to get out of here. Get away from him. You need to take me to the hospital. I'm seeing things. Hallucinating. I think I need medication."

"Calm down. Calm down. We're not going anywhere just yet. Sit down at the table. Alex, would you mind?"

Putting on the pants that were laid out for him, "Wha' is it ye'd like me ta dae?"

"It's not what I want, but it is what must be done. Restrain her."

Brenawyn bolted upright, and pushed past her grandmother. "I will not!"

"Nay. I willna hold her against her will."

"You wanted her to learn, Shaman. This is how she will do it. This is how she must. Hold her and start the change. She needs to feel your bones shift. She must feel it for herself."

"Brenawyn," Alex pleaded, "I willna hurt ye, lass. But let me show ye. It will shed light on things, at least to let ye ken ye aren't daft." She stopped and looked over her shoulder at him, considering.

Alex took this as progress and stepped closer to her, hands held out in supplication. "I willna hold ye against yer will."

She turned to him, eyes wide, and held out a shaky hand.

"Och, lass, everything will be fine. Ye are in no danger from me." Taking her hands, he put them around his waist drawing her closer. "Lay yer ear against my chest. Do ye hear my heart beat?" Brenawyn nodded. "It's fast, is it no'?" Another nod. A small chuckle from him bubbled up, "Aye, that's only from a beautiful woman touching me. Noo listen for th' change."

She gasped when his heart sped up and she tried to pull away, but Alex held her closer. "Put yer hands on my arms, a chuisle."

She did as she was told and she felt the change as soon as it occurred, the temperature change in his limbs, the shifting of mass, the tearing and lengthening of muscle and ligament. As close as she could be to share in the experience of the change, she heard his visceral grunt reverberate in his chest and felt the sweat bead on his skin. She was horrified, appalled at her behavior that warranted this show and yet…and yet, it seemed so familiar.

From behind, Leo made an impatient noise in her throat. "I think that's enough. She'll have questions. See that you answer them. I'll leave you for the night."

With that interruption, Brenawyn was at an arm's distance, and then bereft of his contact as Alex reversed the change. He stepped back a few feet and went through the routine of joint stretches that eased the discomfort of transformation as quickly as possible.

She stepped closer.

"Wait, Brenawyn, gi' me some space for a few minutes."

"I'm sorry, I didn't mean to make you uncomfortable."

"No, it's no' for my comfort, but for yers. Ye see, it's th' blud flow ta th' limbs tha' makes th' change possible, but it flows ta all, uh hem, appendages."

Her eyes flew to his crotch, she could feel the blush burning her cheeks, but had to ask, "the night of the ceremony when I, when I fainted, you carried me back to the house—

"Aye. Ye ha' questions. I kent this would bring them ta th' surface," Alex looked around. "I'll answer them, but first, does yer grandmother keep whiskey? Afore th' night's out, we'll both need th' fortifying strength o' mither's milk."

"The last I saw, she keeps a bottle in the corner cabinet there."

Alex opened the cabinet and laid claim to the Bunnahabhain single malt scotch. "Oh aye, and a verra fine one at tha'." He unscrewed the cap and took a deep swig from the bottle. "Come, ye'll ha' yer answers, whether ye like them or no'."

Alex trudged off to the living room, leaving Brenawyn to follow.

CHAPTER 17

Brenawyn entered the living room with two glasses in hand to find Alex sitting with elbows braced on his knees in the middle of the dainty floral couch. The image was ridiculous, but just as she was about to comment, she caught the look of sheer anguish on his face.

"What's wrong, Alex?"

Closing his eyes and taking another swig of the scotch, he blurted out, "A'm so sairy, Brenawyn. I must ask for yer forgiveness; it willna relieve any o' th' guilt I feel, but ye ha' ta ken I ne'er meant for it ta happen. I wanted ye, true, from th' first moment, but I swear it ne'er entered my mind."

Brenawyn put the glasses down on the coffee

table, "What are you talking about?"

"Yer questions."

"I'm still at a loss."

"I ha' no right. I ha' nothing ta offer ye. Nothing ta offer any woman. I'm no' a man."

"Whoa. Slow down. You are not making any sense. Apologies out of nowhere? Nonsense about things to offer? When did I ask for anything? And not a man? Please. There is plenty of physical evidence to the contrary. You are a glorious specimen of the male physique, I might add."

"Ye are no' helping, woman. Tell me, wha' dae ye remember o' th' other night when I brought ye home from th' park?"

"Well, um, that's the thing, my memory is fuzzy—I told you this before."

"Yes, I ken, but its verra important ta tell me everything ye remember, even th' most bizarre or mundane."

"There were what seemed like voices, not ones that were around me. I heard you at times, and Nana, the crowd some, and Maggie, too. But these seemed to be, you know, in my head. I couldn't understand what they were saying, I don't know, perhaps they were speaking another language, but I felt—how do I put this? Like I was glad that they were there, like I knew them or something; there was something familiar, comforting about them. I guess that's what a person suffering from a dissociative imbalance might feel.

"You know, I always wondered whether someone who was crazy knew if he was crazy. Maybe I am, but I'm getting off the topic. I can ask questions about that and believe me, I *have* questions, but it's the other that really feels pressing, which I need to know first before anything else. That is what I'm having a problem with because my questions are, they revolve around, um, they're of an intimate nature…"

"Aye, and they would be." Alex handed the bottle to her. "Take a dram."

Brenawyn took a tentative sip, and found it slid down her throat without the usual burning, she looked at the bottle. The layer of dust on it showed that it had been in the cabinet for years, all the more time to age. That was the difference between the cheap stuff and this. She took a deeper swallow.

"When you changed in the kitchen, the second time, it triggered a memory that I didn't have before."

"And wha' was it?"

"That it wasn't the first time that I felt you change, the tension building, the temperature of your skin, God, you were feverish."

"Th' first time was in yer room after I brought ye back from th' ceremony."

"That seems to make sense as far as it goes but…"

Alex got up to pace the room, running his hand through his hair, "But wha'? Do ye need me ta say it,

Brenawyn? "

"I surmise that we had sex that night." Brenawyn said matter-of-factly.

Whatever response he was waiting for, it wasn't this. He retreated to the window, "Aye, in th' end, I took ye fast and hard against th' door jamb. I hate myself for it, but it felt so…"

"Sit down, Alex. I'm not accusing you of anything. I wish…"

"Aye, I can imagine wha' ye wish."

Brenawyn sat back on the couch and chuckled, "I wish that I could remember the encounter as more than just a dream."

Alex stopped midstride, "Wha'?"

Brenawyn turned to meet his stare. "You heard me. It's been a long time since I've had sex.

Chapter 18

Cormac paced the sidewalk. The silence veil didn't need too much finesse, just an unbroken circle and force of will. The window was closing. Preparations had to be in readiness. The screen door opened with a squeak, and he chanced a peek around the portico's trellised vines. He wanted to scream in frustration. In a matter of moments they would lose their chance. The proprietress was leaving for the night. If he grabbed her now she'd thwart the plan, bringing the authorities, and possibly Sinclair, into the fray.

The woman rummaged in the tote bag that hung from her shoulder. She let out a long sigh, dropped the bag, and kicked it so that it leaned against the wall, then she disappeared through the front door again.

Cormac felt the veil hum to life, and with it the Oracle and an acolyte appeared from the corner of the establishment. Without a word, the three took up their positions, and from Cormac's vantage point, he saw the woman jump when the doorbell rang. She proceeded out onto the floor, calling out "I'm sorry we're closed for the…"

She stopped abruptly, and looked around the empty store. She went immediately to the wall and flipped on the lights. They illuminated the cases on the far wall and the bistro tables set in front of the bay window. He smiled; telekinesis was such an easy spell and it never failed to stupefy the mindless.

She went to the door and looked outside onto the empty patio and then to the front window to do the same. No one was on the street.

But, I see ye, little mouse! Hurry, come oot noo and play.

Cormac itched to start. The Oracle's methods were unpleasant, but the chase...ah the chase invigorated him. Setting the trap, luring the target, overpowering him, or in this case, her. She wasn't half bad to look at, a little older than he normally went for but still very attractive, and slender, despite the silver in her hair. If only the Oracle let him subdue her, pin her to the ground as the Y-incision was made. Cormac shifted his weight and adjusted himself, grunting. He'd have to find some willing cunt to plow, and soon.

He knew all too well that force would ruin the delicacy of the sacrifice. The Oracle's interlace glowed brighter as she prepared to eradicate all fear, all memory from the target's mind. He'd witnessed it enough times; he didn't have the patience for it himself, but if it led to the end he most desired he'd be an active participant in the eviscerations.

The woman opened the door and peered into the shadows in Cormac's direction, lingered there for a moment, just enough to give him pause that perhaps he'd not layered on the shadows thick enough to avoid detection, but her gaze passed on to a stray cat in the corner of the patio.

She let the door go and locked it behind her and then bent down to the cat to lure it out with food. *By all tha' is holy! She'll ken something's amiss.*

The cat came no further, stopping just short of the edge of the summoned circle that lay undetectable to the mortal eye. Clearly intrigued by what the woman held in her hand, the cat paced the perimeter of the shadow, casting soulful looks and silent meows her way. Cormac glanced at the Oracle, impatience growing. *Not ready yet?*

The woman sat back on her heels and contemplated the cat. Reaching over, she scooped it up with a steady hand under its belly, and the cat screeched and hissed, clawing to get away from her.

Inhaling through her teeth, she let the cat go to suck on her bleeding wrist. The animal vanished through the vines and the wrought iron fence separating the patio from the sidewalk. She called for it but stopped suddenly when she could not hear her own voice—*and all the carefully laid plans go to shit.*

She tried again, louder this time, but nothing. She shook her head, and blew her nose, as if clearing pressure would help.

Cormac felt the air move next to him and he glanced over and saw The Oracle. "I'll handle this," she said.

"Wha' dae ye propose…"

"Shh. Memory workings are difficult." She whispered into her cupped palms, then blew lightly as she extended her fingers toward the panicking woman on the ground. "Watch and see."

The woman sat on her heels for a few seconds more before finally straightening with a struggle. She turned to get the discarded bags by the door and found that they weren't where she had left them. She stood there looking at the bare spot by the front door, unconvinced that the bags weren't there. She went to peer back in the shop and sure enough, the bags were on the counter.

As they stood there watching the woman fumble in her coat pocket for the keys, the Oracle was there. Her gnarled hand grasped the woman's shoulder and swung her around, forcing her back against the door. Breathless, Cormac closed in, but knew instinctively that the woman did not see him. He could feel the waves of the incantation radiating from the Oracle. He took a step back. No need of getting too close and running the risk of being caught in the incantation himself.

Let her work.

"She'll dae," the Oracle commented as she turned away.

The woman muttered, half dazed still, "Do for what?" No response. "Do for what?" she tried to scream again, but with no volume. She retrieved her discarded purse on the ground and dug for her cellphone.

The Oracle signaled for them to crowd her, using the brick walls of the building to limit her movement. Holding up her hand in defense, the woman fumbled with the phone at last. Another unheard scream bubbled up when she saw the blank screen staring back at her. She threw the phone at Cormac. He scoffed at it and smashed it with the heel of his boot.

She staggered back and hit the door. The look on her face was pathetic. Did she actually think the door offered some kind of sanctuary? That she'd manage somehow to lock it from the inside? That the flimsy glass door would hold them off? That she'd get to the safety of the office before they reached her? Cormac almost felt sorry for the deluded woman.

Clawing at the door, she pulled. The door didn't budge.

They snatched her off her feet and towed her back to the center of the patio. A wave of the Oracle's hand sent the wrought iron furniture screeching across the cobblestones to meet its end in twisted metal and shattered glass against the building.

The woman kicked and bit and it took both of them to wrestle her to the ground, the acolyte using his knee to pin her arms high above her head while Cormac straddled her thighs.

The Oracle strode over to squat at her side. The hag patted her like a dog, mumbling hushed words of no meaning as she produced a dagger from the waistband of her skirt. The woman arched against the restraint, "Please, no. Why are you doing this? Why?"

The crone leaned over and sliced through the cotton t-shirt, exposing the woman's abdomen, and then gave the knife to Cormac with a knowing smile. He looked down at the knife and the bare midriff. He grunted in pleasure and repositioned himself to grind her hips down to the cobblestones with his weight.

He lifted the dagger above his head.

No one heard her screams.

~ ~ ~

A strong gust of wind came through the open window of Alex's apartment, filling his nostrils with the scent of blood. The bear coursed through his body and his bones creaked with the anticipation of turning. Grunting with effort to suppress the full transformation, he climbed to his feet, gifted with a heightened sense of smell. Alex grabbed his satchel and raced out the door, his body responding to unknown urgency.

The bakery's portcullis was covered with charred, twisted skeletons of what had been prolifically blooming vines only hours before. The burnt and blackened stems crumbled to ash when Alex brushed by to climb over a pile of scrap metal that was once the patio furniture. The scorch marks on the walls, gouges in the cobblestones, and the shattered glass, would only give the authorities a moment of pause. It would be noted in the report but forgotten. Disturbing enough was the body of the victim.

Alex recognized her immediately. Barbara lay in the middle of the patio awash in moonlight. Organs spilled from her open abdomen and blood congealed in pools around her. The splatter pattern and contorted limbs gave evidence that she had died in agony.

No longer needing the tracking ability, he released the spirit from his blood and turned his attention to the magical runes close to the body drawn in the victim's blood, and the ogham script spelling out the exact words of the curse. From his satchel, Alex removed a half dozen rough quartz crystals each hanging from a leather thong. He dipped each in a different ogham character. Was he too late? He reached out with his senses and felt the residual magic laden in them. The characters glowed,   and   vivid images flashed in his mind, a rest stop bathroom, the image of Brenawyn's face, the stone circle, the Rising Moon—the Vate knows where she is! His heart hammered in his chest and he jerked his head to look in the direction of her house.

Cramming the stones in the bag he allowed the hawk's spirit and keen sight to rise in him and took another look around the patio. Besides the body of a dead cat, nothing else   was   of   interest.

CHAPTER 19

Alex charged up the steps, searching the darkness for danger. With his back to the door he leaned on both doorbell buttons simultaneously. The second floor door burst open; jingling tags and hurried feet crashed down the stairs followed by another set of more cautious footsteps. The door was yanked open, "Oh, Alex. It's you." Brenawyn smoothed back her hair, tucking the stray wisps behind her ears. "Come in." She looked at his pale face and searched his eyes, reaching out a hand to touch his arm. "Wait. What's the matter?"

"Lass, A'm sairy ta call so late. I need ta talk ta yer grandmother. 'Tis an emergency."

The dog nosed his way out the door to greet Alex, but when he sniffed the bag slung on his shoulder, Spencer's hackles went up, a growl rumbling in his throat.

"Stop that, Spencer! What the hell has gotten into you tonight?"

She abandoned the door to nab his collar, but Alex caught her by the arm, "Stay inside. 'Tis dangerous out haur. Let me get th' dog." With that he repositioned the bag and bent to hoist the dog. She held the door open for them. The foyer was a tight squeeze for the three of them, their bodies bumping into each other, making him well aware of how vulnerable she was. That vulnerability had nothing to do with the short cotton robe, opened to reveal a plaid nightshirt that skimmed her knees and worn pink socks that hung bunched on her ankles. The dog squirmed out of his arms and bounded up the stairs, whatever had perturbed him now forgotten.

"He's been like that for the past two hours or so. Barking, growling. It's driving me crazy."

"Animals are more sensitive ta things around them."

Nodding in acquiescence, "It's like he's a different dog since we left Jersey." She pulled herself out of her ruminations, "Well, never mind. Come on up. You'll have to wait; Nana's gone to bed already."

Alex was staring into the curio cabinet of delicate teacups contemplating the vast difference between the woman he knew and the one who collected these dainty wares, when Leo walked out. She was dressed, albeit hastily so, the buttons on her blouse mismatched. She motioned for him to sit opposite her on the couch.

Without preamble, he said, "Barbara Anderson's been murdered."

Leo let out a sharp gasp, holding a shaking hand to her mouth, tears glistening in her eyes. "How?"

He dug in his bag pulling out the six stones. Alex could see the dawning recognition registering confusion and horror as realization struck home. She bolted out of the chair to pace the short length of the room, "No. No. No. No. No."

Alex stared at her back for a moment. It would better to let her piece together the implications, but time was not a luxury they had anymore.

"Where was she killed? How much time do we have?"

"At th' bakery—"

"What?" Leo flew to the window ripping aside the lace curtains to look out at the bakery across the street. The streetlight cast a hazy light on the dead foliage. "But we didn't hear anything."

"They masked th' sacrifice somehow…silenced her…pulled her out o' time, I doonae ken."

"You don't know?"

Alex held up his hands and shook his head, "A'm sairy. I cannae see inta th' minds o' th' Order. Their purposes ha' changed."

"What do you suggest?"

"I'll take her away. A nicht. We'll run. I'll keep her safe."

"Hm. That's if you can get her to go with you. A snowball has a better chance in hell."

"Dae ye doubt me, woman?"

"I know my granddaughter. Short of dragging her kicking and screaming, she won't go. She's still in mourning for a man who's been dead for three years, and she's known you for what? All of three weeks! She doesn't trust herself enough to put any faith in you. Right now she needs to be here. She feels safe here."

"She's no' safe. They ken who and whaur she is."

"Wha…?"

"I was able ta see…remnants."

"How were they able to track her? How far back did you see?"

"A cottage with blue flowering bushes in th' front, I...I... 'tis difficult ta... did she have any issues in years past? Things she couldnae explain? Would she ha' told ye?"

"No, nothing that I recall as being... yes, she would tell me. Why?"

"It doesna matter. She needs ta leave a nicht, if possible."

"She needs to be in one place to hone her skills and form a connection to Tir-Na-Nog."

"Aaricht, then wha' dae ye suggest?" crossing his arms across his chest.

"That she stays here—just for the time being. I'll layer the protection spells surrounding the house. You'll keep an eye on her. Bring those stones; we'll scry for a location."

Alex followed her into the stillroom off the kitchen.

"Could you hang the stones from the hook there? I don't want to run the risk of having the spell contaminated by something the stones came in contact with here."

The walls of the stillroom were lined with thick wooden shelves stuffed with leather bound books, scrolls tightly wrapped in bright ribbons, rough cut gem and semi-precious stones, and the polished edges of geodes twinkling to the light of the single candle she brought with her. The air was scented with lavender, sage, and mint growing in earthenware pots on the window sill, and a variety of herbs hung from the ceiling drying in bunches in the recessed corners of the room, away from the natural light. "Mind your step, there's no electricity in this room," Leo called over her shoulder.

He glanced in surprise at the wall: no light switch or

outlets. A wrought-iron candelabrum hung low from the ceiling. Who was this woman? He hung the stones by their leather cords from an empty plant hook in front of the window.

She carried an armful of white candles, a basin, scrap paper, charcoal, and several folded travel maps, one of which she unfolded, placing it in the middle of the scarred worktable. "This was one of the original buildings and when my husband bought it, the house looked ready to fall around our ears. He fixed it, so handy around the house he was, but he omitted this room in the renovations purposely for me. It was the original dining room."

Alex nodded.

"We'll start with this one and move out from there." She set the candles at equidistant points around the spread map. "I find it easier to scry when an actual street address is involved."

Interested, he looked closer at the map, seeing that it was one of the town and the neighboring municipalities, "I ha' ne'er tried it like this."

"Of course you haven't, because you don't need to with your abilities. Now shush, I need to concentrate." Leo listened to the footsteps upstairs. "I need you to be a distraction if Brenawyn comes down."

"Aye? Wha' should I dae?"

Leo looked at him exasperated. "Go out into the kitchen and fumble around looking for something in the cabinets. You'll figure something out," waving him towards the door.

The last thing Alex saw when closing the door was the

candles bursting to life.

~ ~ ~

Leo sat crossed legged on the tabletop. She reached for a scrap of paper and a piece of artist's charcoal from the basin next to her to quickly write:

Grant to me my desire.
That I may find what I seek
To bring order where there is chaos.

Grant to me my desire
That I may bring the hand of justice
To restore balance where there is pandemonium.

The runes on Leo's arms glowed as she leaned to the flame on her left. The edge of the paper caught and she watched it burn for a moment before placing it in the basin. She placed the first stone by its cord from the S hook set in the middle of the candelabrum.

Once ash was all that remained of her wish, she picked up the bowl and lightly blew over the rim. The flames leapt higher and the hanging stone started to sway as the ash drifted down from the strength of her exhalation. The stone began to rotate, pulling the cord taut once the last of the ash settled on the paper map. It whipped around faster and faster until the twisted cord kinked and the stone was perpendicular to the map. The wrought iron armature, unable to bear the fluid movement, skewed drunkenly. Guttering candles fell, showering Leo and the map with hot wax. She had to scramble to pat out embers that caught on the paper edges.

The cord snapped sending the stone rocketing to the wall. With a soft pop, the books fell to the ground with a thump. Colorful pages of botanical prints, loosed from the books, floated to the ground like leaves on an autumn breeze.

The stone was embedded in the plaster high up on the wall.

~ ~ ~

The lock clicked and the deadbolt slid home, creating an illusion of safety. Brenawyn pressed her hands to the oak frame of the door and watched the retreating forms of the two officers through the glass. They stepped off the porch and began a slow walk across the street. One glanced back at the second floor window of the building and stopped to take out his notepad again. He then turned, remarking to his partner, and pointed at something on the façade of the bakery.

The whirring red and blue lights cast the tangle of dead vines into grotesque shadows. Vehicles pulled up, each adding its own version of flashing lights to the ghoulish panorama, drawing curious eyes from neighboring windows and doors. Yellow police tape and wood sawhorses cordoned off the site to keep the morbid away.

Eyes downcast in a silent prayer, Brenawyn had no desire to see the stretcher reappear with Barbara's body covered heartlessly in a plastic bag. She turned to find Alex sitting on the third step, hunched over with forearms resting on his knees. She reached out to brush a lock of hair away from his face. He looked up, searching intently in her eyes and held out his hands.

Brenawyn guided his hands around her waist stepping between his open legs to hug him. He startled, and she pulled away, embarrassed that she misread his need. She was pulled close at the last, his cheek pressing into her breast with the strength of the embrace.

"Thank ye." Alex whispered as he slid his hands from her waist to caress her arms.

Stepping back, Brenawyn met his gaze, "I didn't do anything." She tapped the outside of his knee, "Scooch over." Gathering the loose robe around her, she sat next to him. Silence reigned as they watched the reflected light play a silent tattoo on the darkness outside the locked door. Silhouettes moved about, punctuated by the occasional burst of radio chatter or a car door slamming. Not until she caught the brief glimpse of a white ambulance pulling away did she look at Alex. "Why her?"

He shrugged his shoulders. "Did ye ken her well?"

"No, not really. I knew her for a long time though. She'd always have a cookie for me. You know the sugar kind with rainbow sprinkles—the kind you need to have a big glass of milk with." Brenawyn glanced up the stairs, "Nana was friends with her. Every Thursday night they went to bingo." She sighed with resignation, "Come on up. No one is going to sleep tonight. The least I can do is offer you a more comfortable place to sit."

~ ~ ~

The singed remnant of the map was crumpled and thrown on the floor, and the residue from the wax drippings congealed on the bare tabletop; both could wait. The open

193

grimoire told her nothing, leaving her to puzzle over why the spell didn't work. She turned at the sound at the door and found Alex surveying the damage.

He entered at her gesture, scooping up the crumpled map and candles to come stand by her side. He followed her gaze and found the stone. "Wha' happened?"

"What does it look like? The spell didn't work." At his insistence, Leo told him what had happened three times, each time spelling out the steps of preparation, the placement of the artifacts, the wording of the written desire to focus the location spell, and the immediate effects of the incantation.

She watched as he moved the rubble of books and papers still on the floor to manageable piles on the counters. He paced the perimeter of the room, grabbing the step stool to set it in the cleared space. The stone was barely visible but he managed to pry it out with his fingertips. He came down and deposited the stone in her open hand.

Leo's looked at the stone, curious to find it warm. "Huh?"

"Tis interesting. How long has th' stone been in th' wall?"

Eyes unfocused, "Let's see. You showed up around 10:15 to tell me about Barbara. We came in here shortly after that."

"The kitchen clock read 10:45 when I left ye in haur."

"Ok. It didn't take long, a few minutes at most, then the police where here for almost an hour—so what's that? About an hour and a half?" They both looked at the stone as she placed it carefully on the table. She slid off the table, hissing through her teeth when too much of her weight landed on her injured foot.

"Leo, this is Auld Magic, veiled ta protect th' source and intent." He grabbed the crumpled map off the table, bunching it into a tighter ball, "It's too elemental ta be relegated ta th' confines of manmade order."

"So what then?"

"Give me th' stones. Scrying is not as effective as it once was, too many people living in close proximity ta each other, but I will try."

"What will you do if you find them? No. It's too dangerous. It would stir up trouble before we're ready for it. Brenawyn would be safer with you close by. She needs to be taught quickly before the Order comes for her."

"Wha' was th' purpose o' this, then?" indicating the ransacked room.

Leo looked at the mess and then at the stones, "I owe it to her. Barbara. Her murderers need to be brought to justice."

"The authorities willna be able ta hold a Vate."

CHAPTER 20

Brenawyn walked in the house led by Spencer, tripping over her bulging luggage, thrown haphazardly by the back door. She stood speechless and confused as tears welled in her eyes. She let the leash go and sat on the largest upright suitcase, feeling dejected, looking around at the scattered bags and boxes. Her garment bag lay over the chair with its zipper stuck two thirds of the way up, white cambric protruding from its teeth.

Aromas of hidden goodies, the lace curtains and placemats, the nubby fibers of the bright kitchen slice under the sink, and memories of many evenings playing Dots with Nana at the table, all made the kitchen so warm and welcoming. The change was subtle, the lace curtains and tabletop decorations remained and the lingering scent of breakfast still hung in the air, but the presence of the bags made it cold and utilitarian.

She was no longer wanted in the house.

The steps creaked, and Brenawyn wiped the tears from her eyes with the hem of her shirt. She sniffled and fumbled with the paper towel roll, knocking it out of its holder; it unrolled across the floor. Spencer entered, his scampering feet sliding across the linoleum. He saw the towels and made a mad dash for his newfound toy. Brenawyn charged after him grabbing the fluttering stream of printed paper. It tore at the perforations, leaving her with several sections as the dog careened around the corner with the rest.

She blew her nose in the wadded up paper towels and turned on her heel find Alex trudging down the stairs carrying her boxes, her makeup bag slung on his shoulder.

Striding over to yank the cardboard box from his hands, "What's going on?" she asked as the contents spilled out from the weakened bottom.

"Brenawyn, wait, I… Bren."

She rounded on him and pushed him, "No, damn it. I don't care who you are or what you can do. Get the hell out."

She saw emotion flash in his eyes and then he was crowding her. Her heart pounded in her chest, "I'm sorry. I should have…I'm sorry." She stepped back desperate to get away until her back hit the bannister. He braced his two arms on the railing imprisoning her. She flinched covering her face with her arms as she turned it away. She opened her eyes when the blow didn't fall and watched him through the corner of her eye, ready to retreat again.

He didn't touch her.

"Lass, did yer husband beat ye?"

Shocked at the question, Brenawyn shook her head, "No. No, of course not."

"Then why?"

He caressed her cheek gently, "Leuk at me, Brenawyn." She looked up at him eyes wide with fear. "That's it. I willna hurt ye. Shhh. I ha' ne'er raised my hand ta a woman. Shhh. All will be well. Yer grandmother is downstairs in th' office, getting th' paperwork in order ta close th' store."

"What? Why?"

"Ye can ask her yerself."

The office door was ajar and the light within cast the shadow of her grandmother ripping open file cabinet drawers.

She poked her head in, "Nana?"

"Oh, Brenawyn," Nana looked around distractedly at the papers strewn across the desk. "Come in and sit down," motioning to the chairs opposite the desk. "Ah, here it is," she exclaimed to no one, and put the paper on the short stack she had on the left corner, the only neat pile amongst the mess. "Alex, I know you are hovering just outside the door. Come in and sit."

Brenawyn got up and moved over as Alex slid past. She avoided his gaze, she wasn't ready to look at him, nor was she going to let him touch her, even in passing.

"I'm closing up the shop. We're going to Tannersville tonight."

"Nana, that's crazy. How can you do that, financially?"

Waving her hand, "Internet sales are the bulk of the business, and the merchandise ships directly from the warehouse."

She stared, dumbfounded that her grandmother was computer savvy. "Really? Wow. Why so early then?"

"With your attack and Barbara's murder, how can you ask that?

"But the cops don't think that the two are related. They're just random violence."

Alex stood by her chair, "Go stand by th' mirror, Brenawyn."

She ignored him.

"Brenawyn," her grandmother intoned, "Do as he says. Go stand by the mirror."

She got up, shocked that her grandmother took the side of this man—a veritable stranger. "Fine." She huffed over to the full length mirror, crossed her arms over her chest, cocked her hip to the side, and waited. "Well? What am I standing here for?"

"Stop acting like a bairn and leuk at me."

She started to turn around and Alex grabbed her hips. "No, leuk at my reflection." He closed his eyes and his nostrils flared with deep measured breaths.

"I'm not acting like a…"

Alex's lids shot open to reveal their burning iridescence. She tried turning, but his hands dug into her hips, keeping her stationary. When she stilled, he took his hand and fastened it on her chin, forcing her to watch their reflection. The urge to fight back rose in her throat like bile and she renewed her struggle in earnest. Clamping her body to him with an arm around her waist, he lifted so her feet dangled inches above the floor. With the other arm he grabbed her wrist, holding her in position so she could see their iridescent runes glowing where they touched. She quieted. Her eyes flew to her waist; she could feel his touch on her bare skin. Her shirt had ridden up exposing part of her rib cage; runes glowed there too.

"Oh my God! Oh God! Let me go. Now." Alex let go and stepped back, allowing Brenawyn time to regain her composure. She stepped away, stretching her shirt down past her hips to cover herself.

Nana was at her side, "Brenawyn, honey, sit down." Leo led her to the chair. "Do you want some water?"

"I want to go home, back to my life—my job, my friends, my house where everything was normal."

"Yer life, no matter whaur, was never normal. Ignorance doesna equate ta normality."

"Yeah, well, ignorance is bliss," she spat. "Ever since I met you, things don't make sense."

"Ugh. Talk to her." Alex demanded before he stormed out.

Nana looked after him, and with a sigh turned back to Brenawyn, who was still seething in the chair. She leaned against the corner of the desk, folded her hands and waited patiently.

"Nana…"

"No. We will talk when you have calmed down."

Annoyed at being treated like a child, she sat back. Things were so much better when all she had to worry about was getting lesson plans in on time and lackadaisical parents who spoiled their belligerent children. She had sold the house and quit the job and what did she have to show for it? She paused when she caught sight of her reflection in the mirror: arms crossed, slouching in the chair, legs crossed at the knee, her foot swinging, *My God, I am acting like a child*. She straightened and rubbed her hands over her face.

Her grandmother's look softened at the change in posture. "We'll be taking two cars, yours and Alex's."

~ ~ ~

Brenawyn trudged up the stairs and found, still on the floor, her things from the cardboard box she had torn from Alex's arms, untouched except for a dark blue velvet pouch Spencer was industriously chewing on. "Stop. Release now." But the dog held on, and when Brenawyn wrested it away from Spencer, her fingers were covered in drool. "Uh, bad boy."

The contents crunched under her fingers as she loosened the drawstring, and a mixed scent assailed her senses. The dog lifted his head, sniffed the air and moved to retrieve his toy. She crinkled her nose, and poured some in her hand; it looked like potpourri but had a scent which she couldn't identify. This wasn't hers.

In fact, as she looked around at the ornate wood box resting on its side, she knew it had come from one of Liam's boxes, one she'd had no time to go through so she had just thrown in the car. She returned the contents to the bag, drew tight the strings, and set it behind her on the stairs. The dog lunged for the discarded sachet, whining and growling as he nosed it on the stair.

She grabbed his snout, "No growling."

Alex marched in holding the blue pouch, but stopped when he saw Brenawyn sitting on the step. "Is this yers?"

"Hmm?" She swiped at her eyes, "No. I don't know what it is."

He threw it onto the counter and tore into the lower cabinets producing a metal bowl. With a clang, he tossed the bowl next to the stove. The ticking of the starter went on for seconds before the burner lit, and Alex held the pouch over the flame until it caught in several places. Curious, Brenawyn met him at the counter and watched his face as the bag and its contents gradually turned to cinders. "T'was a charm, an ill omen tha' has nay power anymore."

CHAPTER 21

The strained squeak of the porch's storm door and heavy footfalls on the steps had Alex and Brenawyn look up in unison. Alex stepped out to shield her as the frame of the kitchen door splintered and two hooded figures rushed in. He inhaled and initiated his shift, ready to fight, but Brenawyn gave a breathless gasp and cowered behind him. Now was not the time to fight, he had to get her to safety. She clasped him about the waist, shaking. He covered her hand in reassurance and moved a leg back. She noticed the shift in his body and moved with him backward in the direction of the front steps. A scream from below gave him pause, but Brenawyn was the insistent one now, yanking on him until another set of footsteps, these with an auditory hitch, sounded on the second set of stairs. They were boxed in. The front was still his choice of an escape. Coming down on an intruder from above would give them a tactical advantage. A plummet down the stairs was far less violent than the hand-to-hand combat awaiting him with these intruders in the confines of the kitchen.

Alex backed up into the hallway, taking Brenawyn with him. The two hooded figures followed, interlace glowing bright on their skin. The one cracked his knuckles, a sneer spreading across his face. Brenawyn was the one to stop now, and Alex spared a glance behind him.

The Vate stood on the landing, supported by Cormac. She was out of breath, but alert and aware.

Brenawyn gulped, "You!"

"Aye, dearie, 'tis me.

Turning to Alex, "This is the woman..."

"He will no' be able ta help ye noo. Come 'ere ta me."

"No."

"Shaman, ye ha' done well. I'll take her from haur. Bring her ta me."

"Nay, I willna." He put a protective arm across Brenawyn's chest.

The Vate's scowl softened, and a toothless smile punctuated her raisin of a face. Her one good eye sparkled, and she chortled. "Resistant ta th' last. Alexander Morgan Sinclair, ye always ha' more piss and vinegar ta ye than blud. After all these years, I'd expected ye ta ha' learned ta respect yer elders, even if it were no' for th' skelpings ye received at yer father's hearth. Thick-heided clout. What o' yer oath as th' Shaman?"

"I could ask ye th' same."

She paused and squinted at him. She placed her hand on the newel post to steady herself, then took her hand from the crook of Cormac's arm. She motioned for Cormac to bring Brenawyn as she shambled into the living room.

Alex saw Cormac begin to move and readied himself. Cormac wasn't going to take her, he resolved, but the two hooded figures seized Alex from behind. He struggled, and recognized John Buchanan, Maggie's abusive boyfriend, as the hood fell back. Alex wound up with his back arched against the boy, an arm braced against his throat. Buchanan was wearing an acolyte's robes and reciting a novice enchantment to garner physical strength. His pride was too big for repetition; as Alex knew he would, he broke off to incite him, "How does it feel, old man?"

The second he broke the cycle, Alex could feel the strength ebb from Buchanan's scrawny arm. Alex renewed his efforts to get free but the other, a more seasoned initiate, was there to subdue him. The two of them forced him into the living room, where the Vate was already perched on the couch. Brenawyn was seated opposite on Cormac's lap, his hand balled in her hair, forcing her to look at the Vate.

The Vate leaned over to dump the contents of the shallow dish on the coffee table. The decorative twig and feathered balls rolled and bounced away. She took out a worn drawstring bag from the voluminous folds of her cloak and emptied the contents in the basin. Alex knew what it was. She was readying herself to rune cast.

She shook the dish to level the sand and drew in it with her index finger, looking at Alex. "Such a shame 'tis tha' ye couldnae be moved. Yer da would be heartbroke ta learn wha' ha' become o' ye."

"Nay, he wouldnae, because he'd ken tha' I deid with honor, upholdin' my oath."

"Haud yer wheest![5] Yer oath! Tcha. Awa' with ye. Ye broke yer oath ta yer caste and th' Order long ago."

Turning to Brenawyn, he said, "Whate'er happens, Brenawyn. I'll come for ye."

---

[5] Be quiet.

The Vate drew the last of the Ogham rune and greedily took the dish in both hands up to her mouth. Like a mother bird regurgitating sustenance for her young, she hocked up phlegm and spit a wad of dark mucus into the dish. A line of spittle ran from the edge of her mouth, but she didn't notice or care. The Vate threw the contents of the dish into the air. The moist sand landed with a thump back in the container. She set it down and scooped it out, packing it with both hands like one would a snowball.

"Leuk priestess, and see. Yer protector is o' nay use ta ye noo."

Brenawyn looked on in disgust, she had no clue what the woman was doing.

The Vate held out her hand, and the clump sat in the middle of her palm slowly rotating on its own. She tossed it in the air, and it hovered inches from her hand, rotating faster. Particles of sand separated from the ball, lengthening and elongating until it appeared as a swirling vortex. The vortex expanded, allowing more space between the particulate until only the rune remained. This the Vate cupped with both her hands, infusing it with more magic until it glowed. "Open his shirt."

Alex struggled against the restraint of the two men, but his shirt was finally laid open from neck to navel. The Vate approached and with both hands pressed the glowing rune onto his chest. Holding it there, she chanted:

> *I bind yer magic, Alexander Sinclair, from shifting*
> *form.*
> *I bind yer magic, Alexander Sinclair, from causing*

harm.

I bind yer magic, Alexander Sinclair, from calling the elements.

I bind yer magic, Alexander Sinclair, from healing.
I bind yer magic, Alexander Sinclair, from protecting.
I say this thee times for the Maiden, the Matron, and the Crone.

I bind yer magic. I bind yer magic. I bind yer magic.

Alex's captors let go as he felt the spell take hold. His limbs felt heavy and lethargic, his chest tight, heart pounding, his muscles weak and spasming. This was what it was to feel mortal.

Brenawyn surged against Cormac's restraining hold. "Let me go, God damn you." She freed her arm and managed to hit him in the jaw, stunning him for a moment, but he overpowered her, and she wound up with her face shoved into the cushions, an arm twisted behind her back.

Cormac pushed on her arm, causing her to yelp in pain. "I understan' tha' an arm oot o' joint hurts verra badly. Dae ye want ta ken for sure?" He pushed on it again, making her whimper and reminding her who was in control. He looked over his shoulder, "Boy, go find something ta bind th' priestess with. And ye, watch him. He's still dangerous."

Buchanan came back into the living room with a roll of duct tape. "I'm going to enjoy this, you bitch." He tore at the end of the tape with his teeth. "Teach you some manners…"

"Yer no' going ta instruct her on one bluddy thing." Cormac had him by the collar, "Just bind her and be quick about it, aye?"

Buchanan bound her wrists as Cormac held her face in the pillows, grabbed her upper arm to help her up. She shrugged him off. She turned and mule kicked Buchanan with such force that he bounced off the opposing wall, blood gushing from his nose. She stood clumsily and ran to Alex tripping so she covered the last few feet sliding on her knees on the hardwood floors.

"Come on, we have to get out of here."

"Aye, tha' we dae." Alex stood and pulled Brenawyn to her feet setting her behind him. The remaining acolyte was the first to engage. He lunged, but Alex feinted to the right and sidestepped the rush. His opponent screamed his frustration and dove for Alex yet again. This time, Alex hit him before he fell, and rained down blows to his head and midsection.

Buchanan waited for his chance, and when Alex was occupied he charged Brenawyn. His face and hands slick with gore from the broken nose, he grappled with her, struggling to get a grip. They pirouetted around ending with Buchanan's back to Alex, his hands crushing Brenawyn's windpipe, watching as her eyes bulged grotesquely. He heard a sickening pop from behind and something hit the floor with a thud. The next thing he knew, he was hoisted off the floor, away from Brenawyn, his arms flailing like a ragdoll.

Thwack!

Cormac brained Alex with a candlestick.

He came to, finding himself lying on the floor with smelling salts being applied by the Vate, who crooned to him. He jerked away from her and sat up to see Brenawyn fully trussed and Cormac pacing.

"There, he's awake. What do you want from me? From us? If I can, I'll willingly give it, just let us go." Brenawyn pleaded.

"Ye will give it, whether ye will it or no'. Ha' nay doubt."

"Why are you doing this?"

"Ah, tha' question has waited six hundred years ta be answered, my lassie." Cormac sat on the arm of the couch. "Shall I tell it, Alex or let ye?"

"Please, Cormac, that is your name, yes? We haven't been introduced, yet you have tried to kill me tonight, and I'm assuming here, several times before, too? Why don't *you* tell me, hm?"

"Och, I like her spirit, Alexander! No wonder ye were so possessive." He got up and caressed her cheek, "If thaur were only time ta properly explore."

Brenawyn pulled away, changing Cormac's demeanor. A frown pressed his features down, blackening his look.

"Ugh, always one ta rhapsodize, get on with it, Cormac, afore my joints get rheumy.

"Six hundred years o' searching for th' priestess, and haur ye are," crowed Cormac. "Th' one ta restore balance."

"What is this balance?"

"Ye doonae ken? She doesnae ken?" he looked incredulous but guffawed at last, shaking his head. "Ooh, Aerten ha' a sense o' humor after all," he said as he wiped his eyes, "Th' balance is distribution o' power."

"I gathered that. I'm not stupid."

Corac smacked her. "Years ago a group was formed when it was made known tha' th' priestess was lost ta time. Myself and Alex, thaur, were made members. Our task was ta protect th' balance until she was found and able ta take her rightful place among th' Druid clergy. Six hundred years is a long time, though, aye? And certain members became accustomed ta a life beyond their means."

Brenawyn's cheek stung and she tasted blood, but she couldn't help herself, "You mean, you became greedy for power."

He surged upon her, "Ye'll never ken wha' 'tis like ta harness such power and ken tha' sometime in th' future ye will be stripped o' it. I willna go back ta serving. Th' gods doonae ken, Aerten herself doesnae ken, what yer capacity is. They're afraid; whauras me? I'm excited. If I complete th' Rite o' th' Phoenix on Samhain, I obtain all o' yer powers, latent abilities and all."

"How do you know I am who you think I am? I don't feel any different than I've felt all my life. What if it's all a mistake?"

"Ah, tha' would be a puzzle, but alas, yer soul ha' been recognized by th' gods. They are ne'er wrong. Ye are th' priestess."

"I'm not familiar with your religion. Your gods are not my God. I don't believe. Yours is not my faith."

Motioning to the hooded figure, Cormac instructed, "Eric, take off yer cloak and gi' her a keek at her handiwork."

The second acolyte approached and unfastened the mantle at his neck. The heavy material pooled on the floor.

He took the hem of his button-down shirt and lifted it over his head.

"And th' bandage too."

He played with edging of a soiled wrap. He hissed through his teeth as he began unwrapping, round and round. The last layers caused him pain as the gauze stuck to the seeping wound. The rotten skin sloughed off and opened sores had bright blood mixing with pus. "Get a good look at what you did to me, bitch." He shoved the arm under her nose. Brenawyn leaned back in the chair she was tied to so that the chair balanced on two legs; she would have fallen over had it not been for the wall. She turned her head forcefully away, but the man placed a heavy hand on the arm of the chair and pushed down. The chair righted itself with a thump, and Brenawyn's head bounced once off the head rest only to come close to ricocheting against the offending arm. The man had the forethought to pull back at the last instant to save himself from an onslaught of new pain to the damaged limb.

Brenawyn turned her head and vomited on herself. Some of the contents of her stomach splashed onto him, and he backhanded her. "Ugh, filthy whore. I'm going to lose my arm, thanks to you."

She looked down and saw the mottled hand and blackened fingertips. "You need to get that looked at, maybe the doctors can save the arm."

"How charitable, the image of compassion."

"I don't know who you are."

"Don't know who I am? He shoved his other wrist at her. She looked down at the tattoo of the three lines.

211

Recognition flared in her.

She looked at Alex. He was trussed like her, at the wrists and ankles with duct tape, in the matching Queen Anne side chair; but Alex was also bound at the elbows, knees and chest, pinning him most effectively to the seat.

"You bastard! You almost killed my dog."

The Oracle stepped forward, pulling the acolyte away. "Enough!" She squatted in front of Brenawyn, "Ye see, ye are th' priestess, regardless o' yer belief system. Ye ha' powers, newly emerged. Who kens why they ha' lay dormant so long? Who kens which abilities will surface? And who kens how strong ye will grow? I ha' nay seen it through th' use o' augury. "

"Please, please, don't hurt me. Don't let him hurt me. Please, I beg of you!"

The Vate patted her hand. "Tis no' personal tha' we must sacrifice ye, but yer fate tha' it must be so."

"Don't go spouting lies. Tell her true, tha' 'tis nothin' more than yer own selfish ambition tha' makes ye act this way. Tha' she will die for naught other than tha'." Alex growled.

"Haud yer wheest, boy," the Vate scolded. "I ha' studied th' prophecies."

"So, ha' I, enough ta ken tha' she's nay mentioned but th' once."

The Vate frowned and reached in her cloak. "*Dun do bheal*[6]." She pulled out a sheathed jeweled knife and tossed it to Cormac. "Ye wanted ta dae him in. Dae it noo, ta stop

---

[6] Shut your mouth

his yammering."

"With pleasure." Cormac unsheathed the wicked looking blade, and Brenawyn yelled out in alarm.

"Alex!"

"Aye, I see it, lass. Dae ye remember what I said?"

"No, I…"

"No matter wha' happens, I will come for ye."

"How?"

"Doesnae matter, noo. Dae ye believe me?"

"Yes, but…"

"No matter wha' happens."

Cormac approached from an angle, the knife gripped in his fist. Alex flexed his muscles against the unyielding restraints, rocking the chair back and forth. The antique wood frame held, despite its protests. In the last instant, he held his breath to await the blade.

"I ha' no finesse like th' Oracle," Cormac grunted with the effort puncturing Alex's abdomen, "but 'tis no' warranted. Ye are no' a sacrifice." He placed a hand on Alex's shoulder.

Through gritted teeth, Alex hissed, "Leuk awa' Brenawyn. Ye doonae want ta see this."

Cormac repositioned himself to give Brenawyn an unobstructed view and laughed. "Dae ye see yer protector noo?" and started sawing the blade through his skin.

Brenawyn screamed as Alex's guts spilled out. "A traitor would be treated verra similar, usually strapped ta a table in th' town's square for e'eryone ta witness. Th' executioner, if he ken his art, would ha' th' man be alive until th' last when he saw was his own beating heart ripped from his chest."

Brenawyn screamed again, pulling at the restraints banging the chair against the wall behind her trying to break the chair.

"We ha' nay time for that, and I ha' nay stomach ta stick my hand in his chest cavity ta yank oot his heart. He'll just ha' ta make dae with this." Cormac took the blade out and at an upward angle sank it to the hilt under his breastbone. Alex spurted blood and slumped.

"Nooooooooooo, damn you!" The interlace on Brenawyn flared to life and the chair broke.

Chapter 22

Alexander floated in an undulating haze, electricity tingling from every nerve ending. He didn't want it to end, he focused on the feeling, tried to relax, but it slipped away. Grunting with the loss he tossed, his limbs slow to respond. He opened his eyes and pulsing colors beset him: reds, blues, so cool against his skin, the feeling came back now, multiplied tenfold centralized to his groin. He moaned. Wet suction, an eager mouth—*Brenawyn.*

He needed her *not* to stop.

The surge of release swept over him and he fought the primal urge to pump into her. He buried his hands in her hair, and she let out a guttural chuckle, renewing her efforts, swirling her tongue over his sensitized tip—

Something wasn't right.

The silken texture of her hair changed, growing coarse and wiry in his hands. He was twisting away, trying to wrench himself from her before his addled mind connected that this was not Brenawyn.

He jerked as a voice to the side purred, "I havena had my fill o' him yet."

The sea of silk crested and broke beaching the voice's owner tight against him. A *dearg due*, the sister of the one still latched on to his shriveled manhood. Creatures of the faerie, single-minded in their lust, they were identical to look at, the only color against their steely gray bodies was the deep pink of sexual excitement. Their puckered nipples and engorged nether lips glistened with moisture.

He vaulted up, reaching for the draped canopy, and yanked. Yards of fabric rained down and the sisters panicked, unable to abide the constriction of the light silk. Releasing him in their struggle to be free, he stumbled away on wobbly legs unable to hold his weight. He went crashing to the floor.

The two screeched and snapped at each other, rending fabric, until one caught sight of him. A violent upheaval left the remnants of the bedding shredded, leaving her sister to claw her way out. She never took her eyes from him. Alex tried to rise, but ended up on his back disoriented and vulnerable. She pounced, straddling his hips. Vicious razor talons raked him from chest to groin, her forked tongue following the same route, lapping up his blood, healing the wounds as she passed. Some errant thought had him tensing the moment the sting dissipated.

A scream ripped from his throat as festering blisters appeared along the path, and she rubbed against him in ecstasy. The sister, now free, swooped down and shoved her tongue in his open mouth. He resisted, bit down, but memories flooded in, a parody of their same position, this time not forced, servicing them both, though they took a more pleasant form. Colleen.

Revulsion and shame swamped him.

"I wonder, if th' priestess saw ye noo, would she be so eager ta save ye?"

Alex sobbed, "Finvarra," straining against their heated advances, "get them off me."

Thunder boomed when the god of the dead clapped his hands. Plaster drifted down from the ceiling, window glass shook in its frames, small ornaments toppled off tabletops, and the *dearg due* sisters looked around, puzzled. "Ladies, if ye will be most kind, I ha' business with this one. I will only take him for a time, ye may play with him more later."

They looked at each other and then down at Alex, but obeyed the god. In passing, he gave them each a caress and watched them sashay through the glamoured wall. "Doonae think about it. Ye will no' be able ta escape tha' way."

"Even if I did, I ha' nay way o' getting oot. It's haur or th' Stalking Grounds, each prison brutal."

"Ye didnae always think so."

"That's as much as ye ken."

"Th' *dearg due* deserve yer pity as much as th' others."

"Wha'?"

"They are shades, vessels holding th' smallest portion of their previous lives, th' most primal, instinctual. Desire is all they feel, but even in their stunted, static existence, they are e'er cognizant o' their confinement. They battle it in their own way, but ye ken this. For a time, ye battled it th' same way."

"Th' way they can change their form ta leuk like—ta get what they want, ta drive ye a little more insane."

Finvarra reached down to touch Alex's temples, "I'll clear yer head o' th' ambrosia's effects."

The room came into focus almost instantly, and he felt the strength returning to his legs as the muscle spasms eased. The sumptuous furnishings of his fishbowl prison came into view. The luxury was lost on him the moment the purpose of the prison had been told to him the first time he was incarcerated here. The view was part of the punishment, to be compelled to watch each target be hunted, captured, and killed quickly or heinously, it didn't matter. This prison was identical, at least from the outside, to all the others lining the perimeter of the Stalking Grounds. He always was returned here to this particular cell.

They were built partly as instructional aids, as if it mattered. Humans against gods—a losing bet every time, even with the resurrections taking him further away from humanity. He was an animal, an abomination to be exterminated.

His head cleared at last and the dire situation in which he had left the other realm came rushing back. He felt the urgency to return.

Finvarra cleared his throat, and turned to reveal Caer Ibormeith who stood silently behind him. He offered her a hand and steered her out of the shadowy recess of the room to stand in front of Alex. She moved with an unearthly grace, a divine ballerina. Her snowy hair was braided and looped into an intricate design, sweeping her hair away from her face. Her violet eyes were strikingly large and expressive, perhaps because she had no mouth, no means of verbal communication.

Caer pantomimed concern for Alex and he slowly stood to show her that concern was not necessary. Empathetic or not, it was not a good idea to be the focus of any god. The last time he had direct contact with her was the night he became the Shaman. He didn't need any more of her empathy; he didn't know if he'd survive it.

She turned her attention to Finvarra, placing a dainty hand on his forearm. He looked at her for a long moment, and Alex was transfixed, watching her changing facial expressions. Finvarra snorted in surprise.

He turned to Alex. "Ye caught her unaware. Ye ha' ta willingly submit ta her inquiry."

"Damn it." He looked out at the moss covered cypress trees growing from the sulfurous bog, mentally preparing himself for the process, "How?"

"She needs ta ken what happened. Let her touch ye."

Alex inhaled sharply and turned to Caer, holding his hands out to her. She took them and gave them a reassuring squeeze, her eyes crinkling at the corners. Her hands were cool in his own clammy ones. She brushed his palms, his inner forearms, and his chest with her fingertips, activating his runes as she went. She cupped his face, fingertips resting just at the temples.

Alex relaxed; there was no pain as he so often encountered with the gods, just a slightly odd sense of closeness.

She threw a glance at Finvarra and he nodded, "Think o' th' most recent events, those tha' ha' ye haur noo."

Alex did as he was instructed, and her grip on his face hardened. Her eyes grew big, creasing her brow, her body stiffened. She exchanged a heated look with Finvarra, to which he announced, "I must leave ye in a moment ta summon Aerten and Taranis. Together, ye will transverse

219

th' veil for Caer ta exact revenge. As th' many times afore, ye will no' be able ta die in th' same manner, but ye will also gain th' gift o' communication as necessary ta understand Caer. Ye will be her retribution. Dae ye ken what I've just told ye?"

"Aye, I dae."

"Prepare yerself, man." Finvarra crossed to the console and picked up a worn piece of leather. He then gave it to Alex who put it in his mouth. His teeth found the all too familiar indents from times past. Inhale. Exhale. Inhale.

Finvarra placed his right hand next to the glowing sigils on Alex's chest, and his left on his forehead. Caer placed her hand over Finvarra's on Alex's head. *"é a thuiscint[7]."*

The smell of burning flesh seared Alex's nasal passages as it traced the bounds of the comprehension spell extending from his base of blue interlace.

Repositioning his hand on Alex' unmarked bicep, Finvarra uttered, *"cosain sinn in am an chatha[8]."* The burning surfaced under Finvarra's hold, creating the scarlet defensive spell. Later, both wounds would revert to the tattooed form of the others, once he was rejoined with his corporeal body, but now it was a mass of blistering abscesses.

Alex let out his breath he hadn't realized he was holding with a grunt. "Finvarra, if we are successful, what little remains free I offer it ta ye, in exchange for hiding

[7] Understand it
[8] Defend us in battle

her."

"Ye would offer th' last o' yerself?"

"Aye. I am bound haur, but when granted leave ta fulfill my office, th' little that 'tis, I offer it ta ye."

"A tempting bargain, but alas I cannae take it."

"I ken what it is ta be indentured, I was born for it, prepared for it. When I took part in th' Phoenix, I kent th' burden o' my responsibilities. Ne'er ta be able ta call a place or a time home, ne'er being able ta take a wife, ha' children for th' eventuality o' watching them get old and die. I ken. Brenawyn doesna.

"Thaur was no choice given. She was manipulated by th' selfishness of others and cosmic forces outside her control, even before she was born. Brenawyn is unprepared. She was born ta a different time. She kens nothing o' being a slave other than historical records. She knows no' th' pain o' having her will broken."

"Is it that bad for ye ta serve us?"

"To break us o' our pride is costly. Most, th' *dearg due* and the *sluagh*, can't survive intact, become shades or worse. I barely survived it and I was raised as a candidate, initiated when I came o' age, served as apprentice ta th' Merlin. It will tear her mind asunder."

"The price has been costly for ye, but dae no' be afeart, it willna be tha' way for her."

"Can ye guarantee this?" Alex demanded, but the god remained quiet. "I thought no'."

"Ye are biased."

"If ye ken what I lost when Colleen shattered th' reliquary, ye wouldnae be so blasé about it. I am forevermore an empty vessel. If th' day comes when I am allowed ta die, I cease ta exist. The eternal reward is denied me because I ha' nay soul." He sighed and pressed his forehead against the cool glass. "For th' rest o' my days, I will serve ye in th' limited capacity o' which I am still able. Reconsider. Thaur is nothing else I ha'.""

"What ye wish is no' in my ability ta give." With that Finvarra turned and disappeared through the wall.

He couldn't tell the passage of time from the light outside the window. Above the trees it was the same light as in Tir-Na-Nog, indirect and bright, but below it barely traversed the thick canopy. What little that did make it through was further swallowed by the thick sheets of moss hanging from the branches. Small ripples from questing fish broke the stagnant stillness of the water, but even that was suddenly quiet as a more menacing shadow undulated just under the surface. If only there were more light, Alex would be able to see what it was that lurked there. Another predator, one he hadn't come in contact with yet. Perhaps it would be its turn the next time he went into the Stalking Grounds.

He paced the length of windows, falling into routine as so many times before. Was it his imagination that saw a wear mark along this path? He's certainly paced it enough over the centuries.

Alex knew he was no longer alone and turned toward his company. Aerten gravitated toward Caer Ibormeith and exchanged greetings, each touching on the heart, lips, eyes, and forehead, and then bowing to the other. They were a match, one without a mouth to say nothing beyond what was prophesied, the other without eyes to see anything beyond the prescribed fate. He felt pity for them because he recognized the chains of servitude. They were nothing if not slaves themselves in their limited omnipotence.

"Is all in readiness?"

A nod from each of the sisters.

"Let us begin."

CHAPTER 23

Pain rattled Brenawyn's teeth, but she was out of time. She shimmied on the floor until her back hit the wall and she was able to get to her knees. The two acolytes pounced, pushing her back.

"Get the fuck off me!" She writhed, trying to buck off one, her teeth sunk into a grappling arm. He pulled back and slapped her. She shrieked her panic, and a deep crack sounded under her. The two paused to look back at the Vate and Cormac, but the cracking continued. The floorboards exploded around them in projectile splinters. Brenawyn's heart leapt and she instinctively raised her hands to cover her face, but the wood rocketed away from her. As soon as she realized she was untouched, she wiggled out from underneath. She got to her feet and assessed. The one who had first attacked her and Spencer sat on his haunches, staring dumbly down at his chest skewered with a broken plank. He touched the edge, incomprehension etched on his face. He collapsed to his side, his breath coming in ragged gasps.

Buchanan fared better, with only minor abrasions to his face and arms. He once again advanced on her, but this time she was more prepared. She found the window sill, and when he came within reach she leaned back and kicked out with both her feet. He dodged the blow, and caught her one leg behind the knee pulling her off her balance. She went down, taking him with her.

Brenawyn felt it this time, a dawning realization, the wood beam, its thickness and tensile strength. She was the one who splintered the boards! She could do the same to the beam! There was a profound groan from the ruined subfloor underneath them and then a loud crack as the centuries old beams gave. Brenawyn fought for advantage. She knew where she was and what awaited them on the first level. Buchanan hit the gondola shelves first and a metallic rending pierced the air as the shelves gave under the combined weight of the two of them plus floor joists, plaster, and lath.

Brenawyn rolled off as soon as he hit and came to a stop at the base of the glass showcase across the aisle. She still had feeling in all of her limbs, and movement too. She approached Buchanan quietly; there was no movement. She kicked his shoe: nothing. Then she looked up. Cormac was peering down at her with a sneer. "Hold, priestess."

"Like Hell I will, you bastard!"

He disappeared and loose plaster rained down, *Shit, he's judging the strength of the remaining floor. Fuck!*

She saw him again seconds later as he swung his legs over the edge, twisting and maneuvering his body so he hung by his arms from the exposed beam.

Brenawyn opened her mouth, but the screech that sounded didn't originate in her lungs. Maggie loped into the storefront from the office brandishing a baseball bat. The small woman mounted the rubble in two bounds and swung for his groin. He dropped like lead onto the heap. She stood over him changing her stance and her grip on the bat to bring it down once, twice—

"Maggie."

She raised the bat again, and Brenawyn yelled, "Maggie, let's go! We have to get out of here."

Maggie looked down at the prone form of Cormac and at the bloodied bat. She threw it away, disgusted with herself. "Oh B, you're okay. Oh, thank God," hugging her. "I saw. I saw what he did. No one was paying attention. I snuck up the back stairs. I…I saw. I couldn't, couldn't help." Hysterics threatened to bubble over.

"Maggie, hey, stay with me. There's no time for you to lose your shit now. Come, find scissors. You have to cut me free."

Maggie ran for the counter, vaulted over it, and grabbed the scissors. Brenawyn turned, as a scraping heavy gait hit the stairs.

"Oh shit. She's still there! Brenawyn—

"Cut faster!"

The tape gave with a snap and Brenawyn twisted her arms to rid herself of the residual restraints. "Where's Leo and Spencer?"

"In the office. B? She was knocked unconscious."

"Fuck!" *We can't get to the front of the store now. The only way out is the back. Shit!* "Ok, we have to take her out the back. Let's move."

She opened the door as Leo was regaining consciousness. "Nana? Nana. We have to go. Maggie, get her other side. Spencer, here boy. Come."

"Brenawyn, Pussy Cat, are you okay?"

"No. I'm not okay. I will probably never be okay again. We GOT to move, now! She'll be down here by now."

"Where's Alex?"

"Come on. We have to go."

Maggie opened the back door and they climbed down the porch steps with little difficulty, but the Vate was there.

"Tis nay use running, priestess. Ye will surrender ta me one way o' other. This way I'll make sure tha' ye doonae suffer."

"Go to hell, bitch!"

"As ye wish."

"Brenawyn, Where's Alex?" Leo asked.

"He's...dead."

"How?"

"What does it matter?"

"How did he die, Brenawyn? It's important."

"He was, um... he was stabbed in the heart after—"

"After? After what? Brenawyn?"

"Damn it! Why is it so fucking important? That woman is trying to kill us."

Maggie held a hand out to Leo. "His gut was sliced open before..."

"Ah, then it's up to us. He cannot be of help."

Leo wasn't making any sense, the blow to the head the probable cause.

The Vate blocked their way out. She had another one of those vortexes floating above her cupped hands.

Brenawyn put a protective arm in front of Leo and

Maggie and stepped out.

"No, Brenawyn. She's too strong for you. You don't know what she is capable of."

"Yes, I do. I saw it upstairs."

Spencer whined at her feet, and she felt for his head. The contact gave her an idea. She knelt down next to her dog, and taking his head in her hand, turned him to stare in his eyes—a move to assert dominance in the animal kingdom, but wasn't that what she intended? How did Alex do it? She wished she'd asked. Shifting: Was she able to do it too?

She took her hand off Spencer but he kept eye contact. She felt different. Muscles a bit achy, lengthening? Whatever it was, it felt like she needed to stretch. Yes, that was it. Her muscles were stretching. Her eyesight—sharper; smell—each spot Spencer urinated in the yard and three separate cats, she could pinpoint. Leo's perspiration; Maggie's fear.

Brenawyn crouched low as the Vate flew at her. As the hag repositioned her hands to propel the binding spell, Brenawyn snagged it out of the air. Her interlace flared and the vortex slowed, coming to a stop and then switching directions, gaining momentum. The Vate stopped, mouth agape. She tried to turn and run, but Brenawyn had her by the neck. She looked at the vortex and with a slight smile, ground it into the crone's clavicle reciting:

I bind your magic from causing harm.
I bind your magic from calling the elements.
I bind your magic from healing.

I bind your magic from protecting.
I say this three times for the Father, the Son, and the
Holy Spirit.
I bind your magic. I bind your magic. I bind your
magic.

A collective gasp—Maggie, stunned surprise; Leo, realization; the Vate, disbelief. The old woman faltered and grasped at Brenawyn as she felt her powers drain. "Nay, it cannae be."

~ ~ ~

From behind the glamoured veil, Alexander Morgan Sinclair stood with Finvarra, Aerten, Caer Ibormeith, and Taranis, observing the scene. Each had an interest in the outcome, but only Alex was spurred to act. "Nay, Shaman," said Taranis, the goddess of death to whom sacrifice was made, physically held him back, "We will observe."

CHAPTER 24

"Brenawyn?" Leo called out. "Brenawyn, honey. We need to go."

She turned her back on the Vate, "Hm?"

"We need to go." Leo indicated upstairs with a tilt of her chin. "Deal with Alex's body. Decide what you're going to do with her."

Brenawyn looked down at her arms, the interlace there had started to dissipate. Try as she might though, she wasn't able to bring it back. It faded further and as it did, her head cleared. She looked about, and frowned. "We can't leave her here. Someone might come. She'll have to come with us. We'll bind her and stick her in one of the rooms."

Once in the apartment, with the Vate squared and squirreled away, Leo issued orders like a drill sergeant. "Maggie, get the shears, a needle and thread in the kitchen drawer. Brenawyn clear the living room floor, we're going to need room to work. We don't have time to waste. He's been dead for more time than I'd like."

Maggie ran back in and dumped all that she'd gathered into Leo's waiting hands as Brenawyn was struggling with the chair to which Alex's corpse was still taped. She laid it back and the damage was in full view: the horror that had been made of a life. She gulped.

"Maggie? Can you help us or are you going to faint?"

She was brought out of her trance. "I...I don't know. I want to help, but..." looking down at the corpse, "what are you going to do?"

"First off, Maggie, things are not as they appear," Leo said this to give assurances. She had no time to spare for histrionics and faintness of heart. Bringing a body back to life was not an easy task, even considering *this* body could regenerate. They didn't have time to wait until he did. Time was of the essence; who knew when there would be another attack.

"Here, let me." Brenawyn took the scissors from her hand and went to work on the duct tape, freeing his upper body with three cuts and divesting him of his shirt to get unencumbered access to the wound. "What do you need?"

"Brenawyn, Maggie, look away. This is going to be gruesome."

"But..."

"Don't argue. There will be plenty for you to do afterwards."

Leo fell to her knees beside the body. Making a face, she scooped up the intestines and visceral matter and began to shove it back into the gaping cavity. "Go to the kitchen, one of you, and find the stock pot. Fill it with hot water. Bring it here when you're done.

She heard Brenawyn rise to do it and give an unintentional dry heave before exiting to the kitchen. "Maggie, thread the needles with double thickness. They're right behind you on the coffee table." Knowing she had to give Maggie something to do to keep her mind off the gore, she added, "Do you still have your lighter?"

"Yes, right here in my pants pocket."

"Thank the gods you didn't listen to me and quit smoking. Today it's coming in useful. Once you have threaded them, run the metal through the flame several times. That's all the sterilization we have time for." Sterilization was an unnecessary step, blood poisoning, an impossibility for an immortal, but it gave her purpose. Brenawyn reentered, hoisting the filled pot.

"Brenawyn, good. Unfortunately, you're going to have to look now. I need you to help. I am going to be occupied with sewing his gut closed, you need to heal the hole in his heart."

"What? I can't do that. No one can."

"There is no time for that. Yes, you can, you did it for Spencer. I'm going to walk you through it. In order for you to heal him, you need to access your runes, specifically those for healing. Do you know how to do that?"

"Um, no," Brenawyn shook her head. Tears glistened in her eyes, "I don't know how I'm supposed to live up to what is expected, what you expect of me. I have this new knowledge, but no practical experience. Seems like I can only summon when I'm afraid, and then it's like it's not me that's doing it. I'm there, but…"

"It's okay, honey. It started that way with me."

Tears spilled, "I almost killed that woman. Oh my God! I did kill John and that other man!"

"All right, Pussy Cat. Calm down and listen to me. You have to put that aside for right now. We need to help Alex. Okay?"

"Yes." Wiping her nose with the back of her hand, "What is it that you need me to do?"

"You have done this already. I am not asking for more than that. You activated your runes to save your pup the night the two of you were attacked. His wound was fatal, the angle and placement right. You saved him. Constricted the blood vessels, forced the healing of the gash opened by the coward's knife, and sped the creation of new blood to replace that which was lost. You did that without any knowledge. You have the ability. Put your hands on my chest."

"What? Why?"

"I am going to activate my runes and I want you to feel what the immediate response is so you can recreate it yourself."

Brenawyn put her hands on her and Leo repositioned them, one over her heart, the other just under the breastbone. She closed her eyes, instructing her to do the same and they sat there. Brenawyn felt her heartbeat thumping strongly and then an electric tingling making her fingers itch, her eyes shot open and Leo's runes were glowing.

She held her hands in place, "Relax, and let be." The itching became more intense and raced up her arms, a glow started in her fingertips, more like the bright translucent skin of a premature infant. She could see the veins and arteries, almost the blood pumping through them by the steady rhythm of her heart. This was replaced by blue luminescent lines interweaving as they shot up the same path as the itching moments before.

"Focus on my heart rate and yours, your breathing and mine, and once they are in sync, take your right hand off of me and place it over Alex's heart."

The steady beat of Leo' heart was reassuring, and it calmed Brenawyn to know that her grandmother's heartrate wasn't elevated. In direct opposition, it felt like hers was going to burst through her chest.

"Relax. You're not going to take your hand off of my heart, it needs to remain there so you can see what one at rest normally feels like. If this was done based off of yours, you'd have him in cardiac arrest when he came to. Not something we want to do. The poor man has been through enough for one evening.

All Brenawyn could do was nod her head in agreement. "Remember what your fingers looked like before the runes started to glow: veins, arteries, delivering blood to the body in pulse with the heart. Imagine it in my body. My blood. Can you sense the vessels? Focus on them."

In her mind's eye she saw what Leo described. Other than pictures she seen in biology textbooks, she had never cared much for learning about biological systems, but she had a clear picture nonetheless.

She felt that, on the outside at least, Nana's skin had a higher temperature from the blood underneath. "Do you feel me getting warmer? That's because I am causing my blood to move to the surface. You are going to do the same in Alex's body. This is going to be difficult because the blood has begun to congeal. You have to get it moving again in order to manipulate it. In order to heal the heart.

"Yes that's it. Don't worry. Blood welling in the open wound is a good thing. It will get messy from here on—

The living room was a bloodbath. Brenawyn snorted, "Like it's been pristine up till now?"

"No, but I don't want to upset you when…"

The blood spurted from the wound, and Brenawyn made a keening cry taking her hand off of his chest.

"Ah, there it is. Okay, I will keep it contained, you concentrate on his heart. Put your hand back on him."

Brenawyn did as she was told.

"Feel for the hole. Send the vessels to repair it. This is just the same as you did for Spencer. Nothing more. Relax. You're doing good. Just a little longer."

Leo felt Brenawyn's pulse. It had resumed a more normal rhythm, so she took her granddaughter's hand off her chest, and clasped it. "See, the blood is no longer spurting. That's a very good thing. Okay, Brenawyn, I'm going to let go of your hand to get the sutures that Maggie has prepared. I will be sewing up the wound to contain everything. Are you okay for me to do this?"

"You're coming back, right?

"Yes, I'll just be going there and back."

Brenawyn nodded, and Leo returned to kneel on the opposite side of Alex. "I'll be quick." She bent to her task. Despite the size, Leo whip stitched the hole shut. "It's not even worthy of a beginning quilter, but it will suffice. He won't even have a scar."

"Really?"

"Yes, you'll see. Rinse your hands in the pot." She reached for the folded crocheted afghan and placed it over the wound, "Maggie, we're going to need your help."

Maggie got to her feet and relief washed across her face when she saw the hideous damage covered. "What do you need me to do?"

"Get the couch cushions and prop up his feet, and wherever you feel comfortable, I need you to place your hands on him."

"I can't do what you do, Leo."

"You don't have to, you're alive and that's enough for this. There are no effects at all for you."

She hesitated, hands hovering over his ankle.

"Yes, you can hold on there. Brenawyn, you're going to place your fingers on his femoral artery, behind his knees. I will be doing chest compressions. You did a fine job at repairing the hole. The worst it over."

"Are you sure?"

"Yes, you'll see. Do you remember the feel of my blood flowing through my veins? Through your veins?"

She nodded.

"Yes? Good. Now we need to recreate that in him in order to start his heart. Okay, listen, this is very important. We have to start slow and build up, I'll regulate the pace, but the moment I say to let him go, you must, because I have to be the one to start his heart."

"How are you going to do that? Do you have a defibrillator downstairs?

"Yes, but its inaccessible now because of the floor's collapse."

"Shit!"

"Relax, all will be well."

Brenawyn took her position, she imagined the blood moving in her own body and willed it to move in the exact same way in his.

"Whoa easy there, relax, it should be a steady increase. Yes, that's more like it. Keep going. Okay, Maggie, take your hands off his leg and move to other side of the room. I don't know what the reaction is going to be but I'd rather have you out of the way, just in case."

Maggie took her hand off of Alex and gave Brenawyn's shoulder a squeeze before moving to the corner of the room.

"Okay, now you, Brenawyn, but stay close."

"What are you going to do?"

Leo shuddered, a sharp intake of breath, leaning back on her heels. Alex's chest lifted off the floor leaving his head and limbs to loll lifelessly. Her hands guided him up as her interlace flared intensely bright. She exhaled, sprang to her feet despite her broken foot and arthritic joints, and bore down on his chest, sending it violently down to the floor. She gave a grunt as she released her magic into him. The interlace faded quickly into his chest, the same pattern oozing through her fingers to cover his chest. When the last had been transferred, she took a stumbling step away and fell against the couch. Brenawyn ran to her, and Leo weakly muttered, "Watch out," pointing to the floor.

Brenawyn avoided the urine puddle, and her heart sank, panic setting in at its mere presence.

~ ~ ~

"Verra interesting, she is." Finvarra mused.

"Aye. Tha' she is. Command o' th' elements, healing,

237

shifting."

"But th' most intriguing is th' way she turned th' Oracle's spell against her. She shouldnae ha' been able ta dae tha'. "

"Because she didna invoke the Mother Goddess?"

"Shaman, has any o' th' order been able ta use another's magic?"

"Nay. No' according ta record."

Finvarra nodded his understanding. "Listen and mark my words. Thaur will be consequences."

Caer reached out to touch Alex and her thoughts invaded his own, *"Tis dangerous haur in this time and place for her. Ye are charged with bringing her back ta train in secrecy."*

"As gifted as the gods ha' made me, she already far exceeds my own abilities, Caer. Wha' dae ye wish me ta teach her?"

Aerten interrupted, "Her bonds will be broken. She wants ye ta see tha' new ones are made. She wants ye ta guard against th' Order. Thaur are still those tha' wish ta use her."

Alex bowed low, "Aye. Yer wish is my command."

"Then go, answer her summons."

Caer stopped him to place her forehead against his as if to offer a blessing; but for Alex a stray thought seeped into his mind, which swirled and coalesced as a warning as sharp as if she spoke it aloud. *"Danger surrounds. Trust neither god nor mortal."*

Chapter 25

Setting his spirit back in his corporeal body was relatively easy, but the weight of gravity was the heaviest to bear and the hardest to acclimate to once the resurrection process started. It wouldn't be as jarring this time, thanks to Brenawyn and Leo's assistance. He wouldn't have to expend any energy to get his heart healed and started, plus, the flesh had already started to warm with the recirculation of blood. He could be on his feet within minutes, feeling only the slightest residual effects, but even those would dissipate soon afterward, twenty-nine minutes at last count.

It took less time each rebirth. He was thankful for that now, enough time had passed for Alex to view his longest stint in the Stalking Grounds with only mild revulsion. His lesson: don't anger the gods. It was ninety-three years until Cernunnos relented and released him. Ninety-three turns on the wheel of time, only getting a reprieve three hundred and seventy-two days for high feast observances. Ninety-three years of being hunted and brought to ground. He went through the resurrection process dozens of times.

Alex lay on the floor, adjusting to his body, listening to the three woman quietly move about the apartment, finishing the last of the preparations. Movement to his right caught his attention. He turned his head to see Brenawyn squat to wipe something off the floor. He felt embarrassed that it was probably his own blood that she was mopping up. He couldn't see her face from this angle so he reached out to place his hand lightly on her knee. She turned and a single tear fell to splash on the back of his hand.

Brenawyn's eyes grew wide and filled with tears. "You're alive!" she breathlessly whispered and immediately started shaking.

"Shh. 'Tis okay. I am haur." He found her hand and pulled her close. She came willingly, turning to stretch out next to him on the floor regardless of the gore. "I told ye I would come for ye."

She touched his cheek, sobbing, "I don't understand how."

Leo paused at the doorway, "Oh, good, you're back. How much time do you think you'll need?"

Brenawyn sat up and regarded Leo disbelievingly. "He just regained…"

"Right noo." Alex sat up. "Thank ye for yer assistance. It cut doon on recovery time."

"There is no time to waste. Someone will come to investigate sooner rather than later, and we need to be gone from this place."

"Aye, we dae." Alex put his hand on his unscarred abdomen. "Th' athame tha' Cormac used ta cut me, is it still haur?"

"Yes, I took it to the kitchen to clean. I'll get it."

By the time Leo returned, Alex was standing, with Brenawyn hovering nearby, shadowing his every move ready to spring to catch him if he stumbled.

He gave her a reassuring smile. "I ken ye doonae understand th' how o' it, but I am solid on my feet."

Leo handed him the sheathed knife. "It looks important."

"Aye, 'tis one o' th' five sacred items o' th' priestess." Both Leo and Alex looked at Brenawyn.

She looked at each in turn, then at the knife extended to her in his open hand. She shook her head, "What am I supposed to do with that?"

"Och, I'll keep it for noo. Whaur did ye put th' Oracle?"

"How did you know?"

Leo exchanged a look with Brenawyn, "She's down in the office. Tied and gagged."

"What are you going to do?"

Alex looked at her grimly, "All will be well. Stay up haur until I call for ye."

Alex passed Maggie on the way down. She gave him a fierce hug and hurried past to get the remainder of the suitcases. Turning, he said, "Maggie, lass, stay up thaur until I say it's safe. Ye kin?"

She nodded her head, holding onto the doorframe, before disappearing around the jamb.

Alex accessed the leopard's senses and reached out to the closed office. Nothing moved within. He approached and saw the door ajar, kicked in from the look of it. The Oracle was gone. He crouched in the hallway and stalked toward the merchandise floor. The ethereal music still played on the speakers, but the effect was eerie now that the place was in shambles.

Alex approached the rubble pile and saw Buchanan, his neck at an impossible angle. There was no sign of Cormac. *Shite.*

This changed the timeline. They'd have to complete the Rite of Widdershins here to be safe, not in Scotland as he intended. Hopefully going back in time to reset the balance would find them at his family's seat. If that were the case then there wouldn't be any cause for concern, but as it was, they could wind up anywhere, anytime. How was he to train her if he knew not whether he'd have the supplies he'd need? How was he to keep her in hiding if he knew not where they'd end up? Still, it was preferable to staying in this time for any length. Cormac and the Oracle were unpredictable now that their purpose was made known, and their followers were an undefined quantity.

Brenawyn met him at the foot of the stairs when he called. She was frightened, he could see.

"Yer car is packed. I need ta get my truck and bags. I would like ye ta accompany me. Is tha' acceptable?"

She nodded her head and was out the door without a second glance. The walk was short, a half a block and a flight of stairs. The apartment was spartan but neat, with the exception of the splintered remains of the coffee table in the center of the living room. "What happened here?"

"Cormac."

Brenawyn panicked and scanned the room, "He was here?"

"Aye, he broke in th' other day. We fought."

She pulled on his arm, "Grab your bags. He could come back anytime."

"I ken why yer afeart, and 'tis wise ta be cautious. We ha' some time. I ken him. He likely has gone off ta lick his wounds. He'll regroup, make nay mistake. He'll come back stronger next time, but it willnae be the day."

Alex stepped around her to lock the door and push the couch against it. "Does tha' make ye feel better? The door is solid oak, locked and bolted.

"Yes, thank you."

"Brenawyn, I'm going to take a shower. Ye can wait haur, the bedroom, och, ye can even sit in th' bathroom. Whaur'er ye are comfortable.

"Oh, okay, um…"

Reading her indecision, Alex took Brenawyn by the hand, and led her down the hall to the bedroom. Alex took the key out of the back of the door. "This room has a lock too. Would ye feel safer if ye locked yerself in haur while I showered? Ye'd ha' th' key and if ye wished ye can push th' dresser in front."

She stopped him and sat on the bed, "The lock on the door here will be sufficient, just hurry."

She opened the bedroom door minutes later to Alex with a towel wrapped around his waist. As appealing as the vision was, his unscarred abdomen contradicted the hideous wound of earlier which was still fresh in her mind. She moved to touch him, but he backed up.

"The blud, it isna yers?"

She held out the shirt tail, "This? No. It's mostly yours actually."

"Aye, ye need ta wash th' blud off ye, too. No' ta scare ye, but th' Vate will be able ta track ye from it. 'Tis a fairly

243

simple spell, all she'd need is a sample o' th' blud."

"Oh, okay, but how?" she pointed, indicating his midsection.

"Ah, ye can inspect and question me all ye want after."

"I don't have a change of clothes."

Alex winked, "Ne'er fear. I'll wrap ye in my kilt."

He donned jeans while she was in the shower, but he was still bare-chested when she reentered the bedroom. His kilt was neatly folded on the end of the bed with a leather belt next to it.

Brenawyn approached and put her hands on his midsection skimming the area where the damage was. "It doesn't hurt?"

"Nay, no' at all."

"So when you come back... I can't believe I'm formulating this question... there's nothing, no remnant?"

"Just the added tattoos as ye can see."

She reached up to trace the newest designs on his chest and arm.

"I'm changed in other ways, but that is a much longer conversation."

Brenawyn's hand remained on his chest. "You're so hot, like an oven."

He sat on the edge of the bed, pulling her on his lap, "Aye, let me warm ye then." His lips touched the edge of her ear and she melted into him. His kisses, feather light, trailed down her neck and across her clavicle.

"Are you sure we're safe here?"

"Aye. Tha' we are, and yer family too."

"For now?"

"Aye, for noo."

She turned to straddle his hips, "Then love me now while we don't have to worry about what tomorrow will bring."

He pulled at the edge of the towel, *"Bheadh grá agam ort riamh, dá mbeadh ach iarraidh orm,"* he said, not daring to say in English that he would love her forever if she but asked. He dipped his head and suckled at her breast. He lay back, taking her with him. His fingers found her slick core, and she rubbed against him. He ripped at his fly, and as soon as he was free, she impaled herself on his engorged shaft. His hands were now on her hips, driving her down, guiding her, but it wasn't enough. In one fluid motion he sat up, claimed her lips, and rolled on top of her as she climaxed, her moans in his ear.

The driving need to spill his seed, to make Brenawyn his, to get her with child, all came flooding in. His tremors started and he moved to withdraw, but her legs clasped his hips, "No, I want you, all of you, inside of me."

"As ye wish."

GLOSSARY

Celtic Gods, Goddesses, and Creatures

Aine: *(AHN yuh)* Irish goddess for fertility
Aerten: *(EYER ten)* Cornish, Welsh goddess of fate
Caer Ibormeith: *(Keer YEW mayth)* Pan-Celtic goddess of dreams and prophecy
Cernunnos: *(KER noo nohs)* Pan-Celtic god of the Hunt
dearg due: *(DAH-ruhg DU-ah)*Irish vampire
Finvarra: *(VEEN varra)* Irish High King of the gods
Nimue: *(NIM oo ay)* Cornish, Welsh goddess of the moon
Sluagh: restless spirits of the dead; in Fate's Hand, embodied as hounds
Taranis: *(TA ran is)* Continental goddess of death to whom sacrifices were offered.
Tir-Na-Nog: *(TIER na noog)* realm of the gods

Gaelic Words and Phrases

a chuisle: (*a khish la*) term of endearment meaning my heart.
Eiliminteach: *(EE le men tie k) Elemental*

Fire Feasts

Samhain: (*SAH wen*) Celebrated on October 31 marking the beginning of winter
Oimelc: (*I melg*) Celebrated on February 1 marking the beginning of spring
Beltaine: (*BEY al TIN ah*) Celebrated on May 1 marking the beginning of summer
Lughnasadh: (*LOO nah sah*) Celebrated on August 1

marking the beginning of autumn

.

PREVIEW
BOOK 2 OF THE CELTIC PROPHECY
RELIQUARY'S CHOICE

Brenawyn covered the pictures, willing them to disappear. Though almost blinded by tears, she uncovered them again to examine them and try to determine the identity of the pretty blonde cradled in her husband's arms on the silent glossy paper. The picture captured the woman's reaction, a hearty laugh at whatever Liam whispered in her ear. The other picture showed her sprawled on a blanket, with a magnolia blossom in her hair. Brenawyn threw the pictures in the trashcan beside the bed. *I won't even think about it. What good would it do? Rage at the possibility? When he never gave me any reason to doubt him?* Disgusted, she grabbed the can and tore into the trash, finding the glossy surfaces, and stormed out to dispose of them. She found the matches, touched it to the photos, and after watching the flame take hold, she tossed the pictures into the empty fireplace.

Ashes.

Appropriate.

She stormed away, but returned just as quickly to watch the last of the embers wink out. She stood there, silently considering the incriminating, albeit circumstantial, evidence. "Ugh. Damn it," slamming her hand on the mantle. "Do you even know that he's dead?"

"Is everything aaricht, *a chuisle*?" She turned to find

Alex sitting in the leather wing chair in the shadowed recess of the room, book on his knee.

Brenawyn's breath hitched as she sighed. "Unpacking the last of the boxes from the house I shared with my husband." She glanced back at the fireplace, "Found some pic…some unexpected things," she amended.

"Ah lass, dae ye want ta talk about it?"

"No, thank you. I'd rather forget it all together."

A few steps into the hall had her at the bedroom door to see garbage strewn on the floor and her dog, Spencer crouched in the corner, chewing a used tissue. "Spencer, put that down!" The dog bolted but Brenawyn wrestled him to the ground, prying his mouth open enough to extract his treat. "Mine!" as she held the wet tissue aloft.

Sitting up, Brenawyn looked around her bedroom, strewn with the contents of the remaining boxes from her home in Jersey that she hadn't had time to go through, now transported here in haste.

"Three years. Three years. If I close my eyes…picking up the phone to hear…seeing the wrecked guard rail, the car…Ugh. Time doesn't heal shit."

Brenawyn reached over for the box of tissues on the nightstand and patted the bed beside her, "Come here, boy. Come on up."

She caught the eighty-pound bundle of wriggling fur. Not content with either licking her face or being as close to her as possible, Spencer did both simultaneously. "Eww, no doggie kisses." She scratched him under his collar. "Who's a good boy?" The dog tried one more time to sneak a last minute kiss that barely missed her open mouth, before giving up and settling down with a grunt as he nestled in, molding his body to her side. Absently she petted him, "You didn't know Liam. He was a good man, even though he was allergic to dogs."

The next item in the box was a small notebook filled with her husband's tight neat script. She leafed through it before recognizing what it was—the notebook that they shared when they took the philosophy class together during their last year of college. How she managed to get an A in the class was still a mystery to her when all she was concerned with was the heat of his body as he sat next to her.

She pulled out the insurance papers she had seen too often. "Again? How many copies did you keep? Did you think I would forget where they were?" She could almost hear his voice. *This is where copies of the insurance papers and the keys to the safety deposit box are...* "How many times did we argue over this?"

Brenawyn dropped the papers, pushed the box across the bed and flung herself back on it, startling the dog. She didn't move until she felt his wet nose nuzzle her arm. "It's okay, Spencer. Talking to you is one thing, but talking to the dead husband... I need to stop that."

Resolved to finish, she picked up the box and extracted the last item in the container, a small wooden box. Brenawyn ran her hand along the ornate brass fittings. Locked. She upended the box. No key. "Hmm." Running her hands along the back revealed a weak hinge. She tried prying the hinge with the edge of her fingernail only to be thwarted when her nail broke. Sucking on the injured finger, she unfolded herself from the bed and climbed over the unmoving dog.

The hinges gave little resistance to the flathead screwdriver. Reaching in, Brenawyn took out a brightly wrapped gift box complete with a silver mylar bow, flattened now after so long. She put the box on the nightstand, hesitant to open it. It was so long since the last time she stumbled upon a surprise like this from a man long dead.

~ ~ ~

Alex paced the room, but Brenawyn didn't return. Keeping an ear to the hallway, he strode over to the fireplace and sifted through the ashes. A soot covered portion of a photo lay in the debris. Centuries may have passed, but Alex would always remember the face of James Morgan. Hatred boiled up from his gut, he needed to hit something.

He got some satisfaction as the brittle paper crumbled in his fist. He wished it were that easy. Jamie never gave him the opportunity. Coward.

A soft cry from the hallway pulled him back into the present and he opened his hand.

Was Jamie her husband? James Liam Morgan McAllister.

Damn him.

Always one step ahead.

Alex stopped at the open doorway to see Brenawyn reaching for a wrapped gift on the nightstand. She fumbled with the paper, ripping at the seams with her teeth until the box was dented. She found purchase and wiped the bit of paper from her lip with one hand as the other pealed the paper away to reveal a black velvet jewelry box. Closing her eyes and holding her breath, she opened the box. He couldn't see what was inside but the facets of the stones spread sparkles across the ceiling as it caught the first rays of the day.

Brenawyn carefully removed the necklace and held it up. She held the medallion as she approached the mirror tracing the detailed design. She looped it around her neck letting the medallion fall between her breasts.

"Years later I'm still finding stuff you left for me? This is why I couldn't live there anymore. I'm trying to move on with my life."

It was only then that she saw him in the doorway. She jumped. "Jesus, you scared me."

"Lass, what's wrong? Is thaur anything I can dae ta help?"

"Eh. It's nothing." Sniffling and wiping her eyes with the back of her hand so hard that she saw spots. "My husband…" shaking her head, "my late husband would give me things, presents, jewelry and other pretty things." She carried the medallion to him, "Three years after his death, I am still finding gifts."

She dropped the necklace in his open hand and whirled to gather the rest of the items back into the box. An exquisite medallion of gold Celtic knot work with ruby, sapphire, emerald, diamond, and topaz gemstones glinted up from his palm. He knew this necklace, could trace the pattern from memory, if he needed more proof to convince him of what he already knew.

"Tis verra beautiful. It reminds me o' another. Come haur. Thaur is something…" Brenawyn straightened and met him, "I am curious about." He looped the necklace around her head lifting her hair so the chain fell again her skin. He stepped back and looked unsatisfied, "The medallion needs ta be in contact with yer skin," and he went to make it so. Brenawyn pulled away blushing, his fingertip loosing contact with her collar.

"Ok, I'll do it, thank you." And she dropped the medallion in her cleavage. "This is very strange. Necklaces are supposed to be worn outside…"

"Humor me." His face must have given something away because her eyes grew wide. "Turn around and leuk in th' mirror."

Much to her surprise, her reflection showed glowing sigils across her clavicle, dimming slightly across her shoulders to almost nothing as they tracked down her upper arms. He saw recognition reflected in her eyes. These were the same iridescent markings as were present in the office's mirror. Alex came up behind her and held her about the waist and the dimmed tracings burst to life, racing down her arms in matching intensity.

"What does this mean?" as she searched his face reflected in the mirror.

"Th' necklace, or rather th' medallion, th' chain has nay power, is *Eiliminteach*, a mythic piece, one o' five, drenched in Druid lore. Five pieces, scattered, hidden, until th' one is revealed. Foci most powerful for th' priestess just as the torc is for th' Shaman.

"Why are the markings activated by it? And why do

they glow brighter at your touch?"

"Th' medallion is a sort o' antenna ta focus your abilities." Eyes burning with desire, he swept aside her tresses and dipped his head so his lips brushed her ear. "My touch is different...are ya sure ye want ta ken, Brenawyn?"

She turned to face him and stepped back to look into his eyes, careful not to touch him.

"We are two halves ta a whole. Shaman, priestess, man, woman, yin, yang, if ye will; we represent balance, and because o' tha' balance, th' gods favor our union."

"If it is as you say, why would my husband have it amongst his belongings."

Everything stopped as the silent weight of her words beat on his heart. "I ken yer husband a while sin." The words were out of his mouth before the decision to tell her registered in his mind. How he would explain his connection to James, he had no clue. The truth? Yeah, as if she would believe him yet.

Brenawyn looked at him, mouth agape. "How... how did you know Liam?"

"He never deserved yer loyalty. He wasna a kind man."

"What? Ye knew him?" Her arms uncrossed so that the robe gaped open. "When?"

"Brenawyn, I shouldnae ha' mentioned it. T'was a long time ago. Perhaps he changed."

"No. Tell me what he was like when you knew him. Please."

"T'was a long time ago. Please. Ye ha' good memories o' him. Mine aren't so. I'd rather no' say."

She moved to bar the door, "No, damn it. Tell me."

"Jamie and I were friends. I ken him as James Morgan—James Liam Morgan McAllister. It doesna matter noo. A woman came between us. We weren't friends any longer. End o' story." Alex brushed by her on his way out of the room, knowing that she was right on his heels.

"Your story lacks detail." Brenawyn caught his arm, "Please, tell me. It's been three years, I can't get over his death. My memories are fading but instead of making it better and allowing me to move on, I feel anxious and panicked, as if there is something important that I've forgotten, but I can't recall it."

"Brenawyn, if ye'll agree ta let it wait, I'll tell ye everything in time."

The backdoor opened with a squeak and Spencer bolted through the room, stepping on Brenawyn's bare foot. She hobbled hopping on one foot, Alex grabbed her forearm to keep her from falling.

"Brenawyn, yer question, ask yerself this, why would he ha' the *Eiliminteach*?

Alex softly closed the door behind him "Why, Jamie? Damn ye." He could have lived with the betrayal; eventually he would have stopped hating them so much if it had been true. Perhaps it was on her part. He'll never know after what Jamie had done to her. Now here he was centuries later with another woman whose memories were violated and altered by the same depraved animal.

Damn him.

All for power.

Not this time.

Alex would give Brenawyn the truth even if she hated

255

him as a result.

Jamie—Ian was dead.

It was time the façade died too.

ACKNOWLEDGEMENTS

Artistic license was used in choosing the gods featured in this novel. While they are all Celtic, they are not from the same country of origin. This was intentional to further diversify names. A list of the gods and their specific origins can be found in the glossary.

There is not much written history on the Druids, so the practices and the clerical hierarchy mentioned here were greatly bolstered by my own imagination. I feel it is important to note that my use of the term acolyte, and its relatives: student, novice, and initiate, are used to describe a lengthy apprenticeship; one that will be explored in greater depth in The Reliquary's Choice: Book Two of the Celtic Prophecy. The term Shaman, though typically understood as originating from another culture, is the correct term to be used here to describe Alexander Sinclair's religious office. Shamanism spans many different cultures and religions, and is thought by some to even predate the Druids.

I would like to acknowledge the anonymous aid I received from the Irish Translation Forum on the Irish Gaelic Translator website. Their translations lend a nuanced authenticity to this novel. The responsibility for any incorrect usage or phrasing falls to me.

While the list of those who supported and encouraged me during the process of writing this novel is long, a special acknowledgement needs to be made to my friend and fellow author, K.W. Penndorf. Without the numerous motivating discussions about plot points, writer's block, and genre issues; the last of which still plague me, Fate's Hand would not have materialized.

Lastly, I would like to acknowledge my family, starting with my husband, Donald Andrew Macfie Jr., whose patience never faltered during the years I worked on this project. He never complained about the hours I would dedicate to writing, particularly at the end when the writing dominated my life insomuch as foregoing sleep. My daughter, Elizabeth, who would listen to me read my newest chapters for hours over the phone when she was away at college. My son, Donald, who was ever so patient with answering endless questions on the male point of view even if it made him uncomfortable. Thank you for your love and support. Please know that you are the first in my thoughts as I wake, and the last as I lay my head on the pillow at night—always.

About the Author

For most of her life, Melissa Macfie has pursued artistic endeavors such as drawing, painting, and sculpting. She holds a M.Ed. in English Education from the Graduate School of Education at Rutgers University, and has spent the last sixteen years as a public school English teacher. She lives in New Jersey with her husband, Donald. Their children, Elizabeth and Donald, are grown and pursuing their own dreams.